For My Boos
I Love You

1

The blood was warm and tasted of copper, like the money of the old people. I didn't have time to spit it out before Maher is coming back towards me swinging his curling blade over his head. I held up my shield, swallowing the blood. I vowed to myself that he will not do that to me again.

"You threw down your sword in the middle of practice", I breathed heavily, "and attacked me with your Urumi. This is your idea of training?"

He laughed. Laughed! His Urumi is 7 blades. Each blade no less than 5 feet and as long as 6 ft. It made my 2 blade Urumi look a little sad, but I can't handle 7 blades...yet.

"Aww, poor Dyana. Do you expect

your opponent to fight you fairly?" Maher mocked in his itty-bitty-baby voice. His words echoed off the walls of the practice chamber.

Still dancing, snaking, worming around me and towards me with his Urumi whipping and lashing, seeking to get around my shield and at my unprotected legs, Maher came. "When they are trying to kill you, will they be so chivalrous?"

His mocking smile, that echo, and the whipping sound of the Urumi breaking the wind around us was maddening. I felt myself losing control. I am in control. I am in control. I think to myself. The constant attack making it hard to concentrate.

"They will try to kill you in the rudest of fashions, I'm afraid". He twisted his face in mock sympathy. The 3 seconds I took to glare at him cost me an almost direct hit to my right thigh. My reinforced fighting leathers softened the blow, but there would be a bruise there later today. "That is the ultimate and most important lesson."

I scampered away from him. Trying my best to keep out of range of the whip action of his Urumi and not become mesmerized by it. It wasn't so hard to become fixated on the quickly lashing blades - the noise that they make when they slash through the air, the way they curled and danced in the hands of their user. Using the Urumi is more like a deadly dance than a straight up fight. Twirling, short and long steps, dips, and jumps become involved when the wielder is well trained.

"Come, my dear. Surely, you have something in your arsenal. I can't believe that the Council would choose someone who is so easily defeated."

"I. Am. Not. Defeated." My right leg feeling heavier than my left, leaving me off balance. I need to wrap this up or I will be defeated. No affirmation is going to change that.

"Oh?" He let the Urumi rest. It's 7 slim blades trailing on the dirt floor. The brass hilt of his Urumi pointed at my head, Maher shrugs, "Well, let's see. You're running away. To be accurate, you're running away when you're not cowering. It looks to me like you've lost."

I stand as solidly as I can muster,

forcing my chest to stop it's heavy panicked heaving, and throw my sword on the ground next to his.

"Yes", Maher thrashes the blades of his Urumi against the ground. "Your choice of weapon must change as the fight changes." He allows me to drop my hands to my waist, unlatching the hilt of my Urumi.

The blades of the Urumi are so slim and flexible they can be worn as an accessory. Whip thin and sharp on all sides, they are dangerous even to the wielder. Even those who train for years can cut themselves quite seriously. I've taken to the curling blade but know better than to call myself master.

"What is it that you call your curling blade? Your Urumi?" Maher presses me. Knowing how annoying his chatter is during our lessons. I've told him a thousand times. He always counters with he'll be quiet when I can beat him.

"Speedy." My hilt completely unfolds with a soft touch to the latch. Drawing Speedy from my waist, I flick my wrist allowing it to uncurl. Speedy comes in at 5 feet long at full extension each blade 3 inches wide. She feels just right in my hand. I chucked my shield at his face and follow it. Whirling and whipping, my blades swinging as I rush him.

"Was I supposed to tell you I was going to throw that?" I force my injured right leg to support me, drawing back to kick him in his chest. The force of the blow running up my leg and into my hips.

Maher's arms flailed at his sides as he tried to regain balance. His own Urumi no longer swinging ungracefully from his thrashing hand. The smug look on his face replaced by one of near panic as he struggles to find balance and regain control of his curling blade at the same time.

Strapping Speedy back around my waist with a quick snap of my wrist, I shift into a tiger and fall on him. My massive left paw holds his right hand down while my right paw crushes into his chest. I roar into his face watching as the saliva from my maw drips from the whiskers around mouth slowly onto his chin.

It's not in any of the literature I have read on tigers - I study up on all the forms I shift into - but I'm pretty sure this tiger was smiling. Catching his eye, I slowly turn my eyes towards his trapped Urumi hand and begin extending my claws. He drops it. <u>Good boy.</u> I think to myself shifting back to my human form and allowing him up.

"Took you long enough." Maher makes a big show of straightening his clothes as the beginnings of a grin grow. He gives me one of his patented Maher winks and opens his arms "Bring it in, Dy. I will advise the Council that you are ready."

2

I couldn't wait to meet Tamra, my Council appointed mentor, for our regularly scheduled Tuesday after training lunch. The streets of New Delphia are normally pretty empty, but today they're full of people getting ready for Christmas. As one of the few holidays of the Old People that we still celebrate - no longer religious, strictly for gift giving and receiving - it brings folks out of their homes into the streets and into an interaction with each other that is as unusual as it is welcome.

I catch a little girl's eye as she approaches with what's probably her Mommy and older brother. Her lips pull back in a huge smile, brown eyes bright, as she almost screams "Merry Christmas" at me. I return her smile full force and wish her the same. She waves her pink mittened hand at that and I slap her 5 as we pass each other. The little girl lets out a squeal of delight that brings laughter from both the mother and brother as they move on.

The shopping bags and the crush of people result in my taking longer than I anticipated to reach my favorite meeting place.   I know Tamra will be on time. She's fanatical about punctuality. These extra few minutes were likely to buy me a 15-minute diatribe about the importance of time as a resource. Not even that could bring me down today. After years of training, I am finally ready to accept an assignment.

The catch sight of Tamra in the window of my favorite little pub, The Light Fantastic.   This pub was the antithesis to other pubs, at least all the ones I've been to, it's bright and airy with windows on 2 sides of the bar, lots of mirrored accents and the best selection of tunes in the city. The place was less of a pub and more of a coffee shoppe with stiff mixed drinks, an impressive selection of Scotch when you were in the mood for dark and Vodkas when the occasion called for light. All of that and they somehow also managed to have some of the most delicious comfort food I'd ever had.

My stomach gurgled quietly in anticipation of one of their hot chicken sandwiches. That soft bun and the ranch dressing on top of the spicy fried chicken breast dressed so simply with a bit of tangy slaw was on my menu 3 to 4 times a week. Don't forget to add the crispy shoestring fries. It would be just like Tam to have ordered for me.

She has a way of anticipating my needs. I guess that's what being a mentor is all about. She was paired with me from the start. A veteran member of the Council and the first Mage I had ever met, Tamra was my rock and probably my first healthy relationship.

Tamra caught sight of me, or maybe my scent. She insisted that everyone even those with no magic other than their sparkling personality had a unique scent. She waved and smiled, holding up her drink as if to say cheers. I wonder if she knows already.

I was just a little disappointed Tamra hadn't ordered the food yet, but that gave me time to share my good news.

"You, my dear, have some very good news!" Tamra says as soon as I get close enough to hear.

"Who told you?"

"Do you mean who told me that your status is being changed to active or who told me about your first assignment?

I shook my head. I must not have heard correctly. "Come again?"

Tam just grinned, putting her finger to her lips.

"Seriously, Tam. If you know something-" I plopped onto my stool not even bothering to take my coat off.

"Something", Tam looked around quizzically. "Let me see" She drummed her fingers lazily on the table. "Do I know something?"

I narrowed my eyes letting a bit of

my tiger out. I could feel the color changing to amber and the figures around me sharpening.

"Take it easy" Tam laughed. "You will be called within 24 hours to be offered the assignment. Do not forget that you can always say no if you don't want to take it. There is no penalty."

I raised my eyebrow which was slightly bushier than it had been a few moments ago. Why would I say no. I had been itching for some action. My training is amazing. The Council has the absolute best teachers in the Realm. The best in all known Realms if you ask them. The curriculum goes from the mundane like understanding the hierarchy of royal courts to the magical arts and everything in between.

"Look, Dy, I know you are rearing to go, but things can get strange on these operations. You should select them carefully based on your strengths, the research you can get your hands on, and whether or not you will have support."

"Seems like you know a lot about this mission and you're not on board." I studied Tam as she suddenly found her snifter to be incredibly interesting. "Why don't you just spit it out?"

"You know that is against the vows."

She's right. I did know. I also kind of didn't care at this moment, but I know she does. I'm likely to be in for a long and boring speech about the importance of our vows and what it means to be blood sworn and blah blah blah.

The waitress interrupted our

silence asking if I'd like a drink and were we ready to order. I looked up; my eyes still amber. Her green eyes met my amber eyes and didn't flinch a bit. I toyed with the idea of letting my incisors grow to see if she would even register it but knowing Tam would go crazy I decide to just ask for another Scotch neat. "Double Midnight Scotch Purple Label* and a Hot Chicken Sandwich. Extra crisp on those fries, please." The girl nods her understanding and takes Tam's order.

Tam meets my eyes as the girl walks away. "What are you doing?" Her voice is nearly imperceptible amongst the other noises of the pub. While I'm still trying to decide between playing innocent or ignoring the question altogether, she asks it again. This time I only hear it in my mind. I know she's serious.

"Tam," I say in my most soothing voice, "they never notice anything. That's why we live amongst them. Unbothered."

The incredulity in her gaze causes me to rush on, "If there's one thing you can trust, it's that the Giftless will be blind to what's in front of them."

Tam shook her head. "You don't know what to trust and that makes you dangerous."

"To myself?" I asked playfully.

"To everyone." Tam's flat reply resonated in my ears for the entirety of our lunch. It nearly spoiled the taste of the sandwich. Nearly.

3

The air was still chilly when we leave The Light Fantastic. It's not quite as enjoyable as before Tam's commentary about trust, but it ain't bad. That's for sure. Despite what Tamra thinks, I'm up for whatever the Council has to offer me. It will be my first and to top it off it must really be something special if it's got Tam's panties twisted. It's not like her to be snippy, at least not with me.

I'm not going to let Tam change my mood today. What I need is some time to think and most definitely a nap. I'm too excited to sleep now, a run would take care of that, but I can feel that my body is tired. The run might actually need to be a fast paced walk. I head for

Sweet Park.   It's my favorite public place.

We learned from the Old People how important it is to preserve the natural environment. Since the establishment of the New World Administration, the Realm-wide government that replaced the disaster that presided over our Realm for the previous 200 years, almost everything is made of organic materials. There is very little concrete in our parks, the benches are made of renewable products, the facilities are impeccable, and there is always staff on hand ensuring that the park stays that way.

The park is already decorated for Christmas and is full of people enjoying them. There are couples holding hands, gazing at one another as often as they gaze at the holiday tree lights and just as fondly. There are kids and adults on the small ice-skating rink which to me is the real draw during the winter. The poor teens working their holiday jobs as Santa's Ice Skating Elves must go home with bruises from head to toe.

The staff decked out in their festive holiday costumes bustle about on the ice helping those who have fallen and trying to keep collisions from happening. All of this while attempting to maintain their own footing. I grab a seat on one of the benches and prepare to take in the show.

"May I join you?" I hear from a voice next to me. From the feel of the bench settling, it seems that was a rhetorical question. His scent was strong a cool autumn night - crisp, clean, and laden with freshly fallen leaves. I could scent him without even trying. A magical being then, and a powerful one. This would be interesting.

"Doesn't seem that I can stop you." I only half joked trying not to allow my body to tense. I spare him a look over my shoulder and decided to engage a bit more when I laid eyes on him. Sun kissed skin, dark brown eyes, and thick sexy lips wrapped up in a black wool coat, creamy bone colored hat and scarf. His hands were in his pockets, but I was certain that he wore matching gloves. He was put together. No doubt about that.

He gave me a little nod of concession before turning his attention towards the main attraction out on the ice. I don't think anyone would pick such a public place to come after me. This was something else entirely. I wanted to know what, but I was in no rush. We could play this little game for a while.

One of the elves was in the middle of a fallen skater sandwich that was directly in the way of a group of wobbly skaters.

"This is not going to end well." My new companion commented flatly bringing a smile to my lips before I could suppress it.

It looked like the wobbly skaters were trying their best to navigate around the sprawl of arms and legs on the ice in front of them. The first three were safely going by on the left side and the fourth one was approaching the flank crossing her left leg over her right in attempts to change her trajectory. She wasn't moving fast enough and three others in her group were right behind her and a bit more adept at change. The first skater tripped over an outstretched leg and started the tumble chain for her group.

The poor elf got the brunt of it. On top of her legs were the original two, on top of her torso was a new one, and on top of that one another one was coming windmilling arms not withstanding it was going to end with that one on the very top. Somehow the skater under the elf had managed to escape and was trying desperately to get out of the new melee. The windmill caught him as he tried to break away toppling him to the ground achingly close to the poor elf's head.

"She might want to rethink her Holiday job." I managed to choke out between laughs.

My stranger/friend was also laughing. His laugh was wonderfully deep and full. Full in the way that little girl's squeal had been. It was full of joy. "I don't know if we should be taking this much joy in this."

He shrugged, "It's Christmas. 'Tis the season of joy." This brought a new peal of laughter from both of us.

I guess it wasn't so bad to have a stranger's company on a cold day at the park even if it wasn't strictly a coincidence.

"I'm going to grab a hot cocoa and

come back for more of the show." I stood up never taking my eyes from what was now boasting 3 elves to 8 very poor ice skaters ratio. I waffled on whether to extend the invitation and decided what the hell, "Want some?"

"Sounds good."

I watched as he lifted what was probably 230 lbs of solidness packed into a 6'3" frame from the bench. He moved easily and confidently, extending his left arm then crooking it into a nook for my arm.

"I think I'll keep both arms free until you tell me who you are." I said amicably.

I was impressed by the way he held his face. He neither looked surprised nor disappointed that his little jig was up.

Straightening his arm, he bent his head in an as-you-wish gesture, gave a quick flourish with his right hand and said, "I am called Tomas."

"I am sure you already know what I am called."

"You are called the OmniShifter by power, Dyana by name, and beautiful in my estimation."

"And what is your real name Tomas?" I rolled my eyes both before and after asking the question.

"Would I tell a stranger and let them weild the power of my secret name over me."

"You would tell an ally."

"Now, now, Dyana. Let's not get ahead of ourselves."

"And let's not play anymore games."

I was beginning to get a bit impatient. This dude was encroaching on my me time with this nonsense and I could see from here the pile up on the ice was getting worse and I was missing it.

"While we're at it. Are you going to let me see what you really are? This is not your true form is it?" He had the nerve to look pleased by my assessment.

"Not at this time, Dyana. Not at this time." He again crooked his arm, looking pointedly from it to me and back again.

I stepped forward taking his arm the wool of the coat prickly against my bare fingers. His scent was intoxicating. I fought not to shake my head. I couldn't let this guys see the way he was affecting me. I don't think he's even trying.

"Way to ruin a great afternoon." I grumbled.

"On the contrary, I think you will find this afternoon much improved." Just as he said it, I recognized what was causing this feeling of intoxication and knew it was too late to let go. I might be lost between the Realms forever if I did. Tomas was a World Walker and we were going for a jaunt.

4

My free hand instinctively reached for the hilt of my curling blade. The blade wrapped around my full-length leather trench's waist. It looked to all the world like a fancy if eccentric belt. Tomas or whatever his name was would feel its fury if this little unplanned trip turned out to be foul.

No need to worry, Dyana. I heard him say directly in my mind. The words interrupting my thoughts.

How very forward of you. I sent to him making sure to keep my mental voice as still and calm as I would have made my aural voice. I don't recall opening my mind to you.

He laughed that full deep laugh into my mind. *You didn't close it either.*

It made me smile as annoyed as I was, I couldn't help but smile at it. I allowed the smile to reach my lips and brought it forward in my mind as I covertly attempted to dig into his mind. *Word play. What other tricks are up your sleeve?*

I knew of World Walking from my
studies with the Council. The seconds
between the worlds were the most
dangerous of the entire trip. They could
be marked by queasiness for the rider,
but the walker would feel only a rush of
energy and emotion something akin to what
the Old People called "a high". It could
be addictive both to the rider and the
walker. After making their first trip,
many change. They crave only to travel
from world to world, never stopping,
never landing, never living a life inside
of any one time and space. Those who
fall into that trap are often lost
between worlds, floating and feeling high
until they die. In death, their body is
said to disburse, and their chakra

energies are absorbed into the abyss that is all creation.

The headiness was beginning to go away and the feeling of motion even as we stood still began to abate as well. We must have reached our destination. I closed my mind to Tomas and any who might be around. How foolish of me to have let my guard down in the first place. What was my problem? I felt a push toward my mind. It was gentle and I knew it was Tomas asking permission. I opened to him just a bit.

We are in the Council's 3rd chamber.

I turned to face him, making sure to keep contact in case I was wrong about the jaunt being over.

How? My broadcast was a little more strongly than I would have preferred. I knew my reaction could give away much, but I had never been inside the Council's chambers. The chambers were off limits unless one was explicitly summoned. I was very near panicked.

I asked Ashka if I could be the one to bring you here. He began to change as I looked at him. The elaborate glamour that he had been casting falling away bit by bit. The scratchy wool under my fingers became warm flesh. His dark brown eyes becoming lighter under they came to their final rest on a beautiful reddish tone, almost the color of amber. His skin was also changing, it's color deepening from the sun kissed, to bronze, and finally resting just short of copper. If the sunset was a person, it would have been Tomas.

His snug wool hat now gone and replaced by close cut hair of auburn hue. His ears were a study in shapes - elongated at the top and almost imperceptibly pointed while the conch interior was outlined by a curl of skin like a typical human ear and a lobe about 1/2 the size of the extended top of the ear. The lips, they were still the same. The mouth almost pouty under his broad nose. I fought to keep my mind shielded as I took in what had to be the most beautiful man I'd ever seen. No not man, but beautiful for sure. I couldn't stop my eyes from widening as I realized that he was Fae.

I felt the soft push toward my mind. I allowed it entrance and heard him say *Dyana, I am Prince Tomas of the Court of*

Dusk. I am here on behalf of the Courts of the Fae Realm. We are in need of the Council's assistance.

Why do you need assistance? My assistance?

It is for the Council to decide what you need to know, not me.

Then why did you come to get me? Why did the Council allow such interference from an outsider? Where are they? Where is is Ashka?_

I stopped my barrage of questions long enough to look around me. We were in a dark room softly lit by sparse arrangements of candles. There were pillows of varying sizes littering the floor in a half circle, some as small as a throw pillow, some big enough to fit a whole person, and many sizes in between.

A slightly raised area in the middle of the soft circle backed onto the wall. It was raised just enough so that those who sat around it could see who or what was on the circle, but not be dwarfed by it.

Are we in the Council Room? Even my thought was a reverent whisper.

I didn't need an answer. I knew where we were. I allowed my hand to drop from Speedy's hilt, let go of the prince's arm, and turned to face the center of the circle. I had only seen this place in the astral plane.

When I first began to shift. I was terrified and utterly alone. At first, I thought it was just a dream as I often woke up with torn sheets and half formed memories. Then I began abruptly leaving arguments as I felt my hands curling up into claws and the *hackles on my back raising and knew that it wasn't something I was dreaming. It also might have been something that I couldn't control. I ignored Ashka's calls at first. The soft whisper of my name in my mind, sometimes soft sometimes more loudly. I ignored it for weeks, months maybe. One day as I lay between the land of dreams and the world of the waking when we are most naturally open to the astral plane, I allowed myself to follow the voice. I had followed it here to this room. Followed it here to the inner chamber.

After months of ignoring the voice beckoning me to the space between worlds, a voice that I thought was just another sign of the crazytown I was on a trip towards, I allowed myself to answer the call. What or rather who (or maybe it is what) called to me referring to itself as Ashka. It offered me an opportunity to be with those who had powers outside the realm of human understanding.

Ashka offered me a chance to be part of something. I was offered the chance to be of service to the known Realms and I took it. She had given me the sweet knowledge that there were others like me and to opportunity to learn how to use my gifts. and other things

Turning slowly toward the prince, hand again resting on Speedy, I asked flatly, "Where are they?"

He nudged softly at my mind again. I let down my guard the smallest of bits. *They are here, Dyana. You must calm down and see._*

I immediately closed my mind to him. These thoughts were not for him. My confusion was obvious, I'm sure, he didn't need to know my exact thoughts too. He gestured to the circle and nudged again.

Once more I allowed him to speak to me in words only we two could know, *Please sit with us and all will be explained.*

Drawing in a long cleansing breath, I relaxed my body and willed my mind to follow. I exhaled slowly, deeply, allowing my whole self to release with the exhale. Walking to the outermost half of the Council's circle, fighting the desire to jump into the soft pool of pillows, I leisurely - or as leisurely as my still beating a mile a minute heart would allow - sat down on the nest of pillows. I motioned for the Prince to sit at my left. He smiled, amber eyes glowing in the soft light. He was magnificent, but I would not be distracted. Not now. Not on my first visit to the Chamber of the Council.

Closing my eyes and allowing my other senses to take over, I felt him settle in next to me. His scent soft now and oddly reassuring. I steadied myself, regaining control of my chakra, reigning in the energy that had begun to race as quickly as my heart at this sudden change of venue and events. My chakra once again flowed smoothly through its points. I could feel that there were others present here. They had been hidden when I was scattered, but I could sense they had been here all the while. Observing, judging, and they had somehow found me worthy even after my little freak out. They found me worthy and I was sitting amongst them. I was sitting amongst the Council.

I heard the voice of Ashka both in my mind and in my ears. She spoke softly, but it was still disconcerting to hear both ways. I steadied myself again focusing on her words and not the strange feeling, willing my chakra to remain calm and focused. I am ready. It is so.

"Welcome", Ashka repeated.

I am honored.

"The Prince has brought you to us for you to receive the Fae Realm's request for assistance. You need not

feel compelled to assist, nor fear repercussion should you decide against collaboration." Ashka turned her head slightly to face the Prince. The other members of the council faced him as well.

The Prince did not bother with nudging this time. He spoke as Ashka had, aloud and in my mind. "*There is an as yet unidentified threat to one of the Court of Dusk's most beloved artifacts. We believe that someone is trying to steal it.*"__

"An artifact? What type of artifact?"

Apparently, I had spoken instead of just wondered because the Prince answered, "*I am unable to tell you everything. We believe that the less you know about the artifact, the safer it and you will be."*

I couldn't be sure, but I thought the last bit had only been to me. I wondered if the others had heard that little bit of nonsense too.

"The time is short before the Festival of the Winter Solstice and that is the time that we believe the artifact will be stolen."

Ashka picked up where the Prince had left off. *"The Fae have requested four members of the Council to enter their realm and be aware. We have given them the choice of 3 shifters, and they have rested on you Dyana, OmniShifter, blood sworn to the Council."*

I nodded my head in ascent and she continued, *"You will enter their Realm as a guest of the Night Queen."*

I could not control the gasp that I let out. Thankfully, Ashka paused allowing my rushing thoughts to run their course.

I knew that Fae existed; however, the literature about them is sparse to say the least. They do not trust the Realm of Men and forbid any knowledge of them be given other than what they have allowed to reach this world. It is only those who are part of the Gifted of the Realm who even know for sure they exist. Even among us Gifted the Night Queen is little more than a myth - a queen with dark skin like the night sky. My eyes flew to the Prince again and I thought how I had immediately likened him to the sunset.

It is an honor. I finally manage

to get out. It was certainly an honor and one that I wasn't really sure I was up for.

Ashka continued, *"You will enter the Court as one of the Fae. Your position will be to simply observe. If anything or anyone seems out of place, you are to report them to the Prince. All Courts of the Fae know we are sending 4 of ours to them; however, your safety is only guaranteed as long as you obey the rules of the Fae. They are the same as our own. Is this understood?"*

The rules of the Council were simple, honor and the truth first and always. I nod my head in accord and feel rather than hear the agreement of the Council members in the chamber.

"You are free to change your mind

any time prior to entering the Fae Realm. Once there, you have chosen. "The sound of Ashka in my ears and mind grew dim and the feeling of headiness began again. No! I wasn't ready to go. There was so much more I wanted to see, ask, know about the Council. I turned to the Prince to tell him to stop, but he was no longer there.

"*I am sending you home for now. The Prince will collect you tomorrow.*" Ashka's voice reverberated in my mind.

Holy Shai! I think as I barrel through the nothingness between worlds into my own. Ashka's power is both amazing and terrifying.

5

My walk from the park had gone by in a flash. The folks I passed on the streets, the carolers going door to door singing about Santa and his reindeer, even the want to be pick pocket who I had stopped with just a look weren't enough to fully get me out of my own head. I had been in the astral plane. I had physically been present in a non-physical place. What does that even mean? How was it possible? Do I even understand what the astral plane is? I had more questions now than before. There was so much I didn't know.

I'm not sure if I sensed her before I saw her or if I just knew she would be there, but I knew Tamra would be waiting at my front door when I turned the corner. Although I live in Center City, my block is completely residential. It's unusual for there to be more than 5 people on it at any one time and today was no different. Her plush red beanie with the giant pom on top was not hard to spot.

I wasn't sure what kind of visit it was going to be. Was I going to get more of the big sister talk or were we going to talk like friends? To me it didn't much matter either way. She was going to get an earful of what happened like it or not.

Tam spotted me and began walking towards me, her gait a little quicker than normal. When she got a few feet away from me, she looked shaken a bit. Her eyes darted around me as if looking for something just to the right or left of me. When she got within arm's reach, she pulled me into a hug that was strong enough to take my breath away.

"Nice to see you too." I choked out returning the hug just as hard as she was giving it. She held me out at arm's length, her eyes no longer darting but focused on mine. She pulled me back into a hug that was a little less intense than the first one, sighed, and let me go. Her arms falling to her sides as she took a step back.

"What is it, Tam?"

"I came looking for you. I followed your scent to the park and it seemed to just stop there. I came here and you weren't here either.."She trailed off, her eyes slowly widening. "Where have you been?"

"You might need a scotch to accompany this story." I grin at her.

Tam sat on the edge of my most comfy chair, the tan leather deal that managed to be simultaneously over-stuffed soft and firm in all the right places. She had sat in the same position for over 25 minutes as I told her the story. Tam sipped from her Double Midnight, pouring more as the story got stranger and stranger. At one point I thought she was going to drop her glass all over my electric blue wool rug, but she just leaned back in the chair exclaimed 'Holy Shai' took up her original position again and urged me to tell more.

When I got to the end and finally

stopped my pacing, I was still too pumped to sit down. I made myself a drink and settle on a standing position beside my wood burning fireplace. Back against the cool wall, and the heat of the Double Midnight running down my throat give me a sense of place that I hadn't been feeling since the first realization that the Prince was taking me on a jaunt.

I wanted to hear Tam's thoughts, but I didn't want to rush her. Hell, it had happened to me and I didn't know how to voice my thoughts about it even to myself. I took up my pacing path again. Going from the peninsula that separated the kitchen space from the living room, crossing the fireplace and couch, walking to the left of the comfy chair and settling on the window seat for a more second. Before my bottom even put a dent a in the bench pillow or tousled the throw, I was back up again.

"For the love of Shai and all the Fates, Dy. Sit it down. All your jittering on top of the story is more than I can take."

I stick my tongue out at her but am so happy that she is saying something. I need her to talk to distract me from what's happened from the crazy thing that I am about to do tomorrow.

"Have you been to the Council's Chamber before?"

"What? Why did you let me believe that it was a non-physical realm?"

"The Council chooses what you know about the astral plane, not me."

I look at her not attempting to

hide my incredulity that was bordering on aggravation. How could she have not told me something so vital about the Council. What else might she not be telling me?

"Don't give me that look." Tam's tone was the same one that she used when I was tired of being pushed at practice or had it up to here with being assigned three books on anatomy and physiology to read and be tested on with only two weeks to prepare. The tone said just be cool. But this was not like those times. Not one bit. I turned my back to her, feeling my fingers tingling. They wanted to curl into claws.

"I'm going to ask you again," I damn near growl, "Why didn't you tell me?"

I feel the nudge at my mind and know that Tam is trying to show me something.

I didn't even realize that I had sealed it so tightly again. Normally I leave holes in my defense for those who I would like to connect with, but I had closed Tam out without even thinking about it.

I open a snippet allowing Tam's thoughts to connect directly with me. I turn to face her. The fire warm against the back of my legs and my still curled fingers grounding me. *This better be good.* I sent to her.

She assures me, *It is.*

In my mind's eye, I see a young Tam looking into a mirror. She's talking to it. No, not quite talking to it but at it. I concentrate on hearing her. She's reciting the Councils credo "Honor and truth - first and always" again and again.

So, she's always been a weirdo, I laughed to myself and fought to stay focused on the projection.

The room was way more girly than any place I would imagine Tam living before her entry into the Council or after. She'd been a part of the Council for 8 years or at least that was what I thought, but this version of her could not have been more than 12 years old. In my estimation Tamra would be at least 10 years off joining the Council.

The girl gets up. Her pink fingernails and toes almost the same shade as her wall, she drags herself over to her tall white dresser and carefully places the hand mirror on top. The room is immaculate. The white carpet totally bereft of any visible dirt. Young Tamra's bed is decked out in an arrangement of pillows and stuffed animals over a fluffy looking white comforter. Tamra falls out onto the bed. Laying with her feet dangling off the edge. Her head nestled between a pink elephant and a yellow throw pillow, Young Tam closes her eyes and begins to cry.

Okay, what am I watching here, Tam? I ask losing my patience.

*Just watch,*_she answers.

The room is darkening. I look at the pink clock on the wall. It's only 5p. Way too early for it to be getting dark on what looks like a fine spring day. And it's a weird kind of darkening. The light is almost being sucked out of the room. I realize it is being drawn from the room. It's being drawn from the room

and into the figure on the bed.

   The figure is rising from the bed,

light beneath and around it as if on a

cushion of light. Tam's eyes must be

open because now there are 2 beams of

light hitting the ceiling above her face.

The light around her is glowing brighter

and brighter. Even in my mind's eye, I

want to turn away to protect myself from

seeing it. Just before I turn, the light

in the room returns to normal and the

girl plunks back onto her bed.

   Seriously,Tam? We have time for

this? I pushed Tamra from my mind and

once again we were just 2 people chatting

in a living room. Tam was doing her best

to remain serious, but the edges of her

lips are clearly itching to twist into a

grin.

"Look, Dy. You know that we are all Walkers of Worlds, right? All of us who are blood sworn. It's part of why we are allowed to be blood sworn."

I knew, of course I knew. "But, I.."

"-you have never done it on your own." Tamra finished for me. "It is because you don't believe you can, Dy."

"Whatever, Tam. If you don't have some actual information for me instead of fake memories, I'm going to have to ask you to leave." I pause for dramatic effect, fluffing my black curls, and looked her dead in the eye, "I've got a date with a Prince tomorrow".

Tam rolls her eyes and lets out the giggles that have been brewing since she sent the false memory to my mind. "I do have useful information. I've only been to the Fae Realm 3 times, but I have made some observations that I think you should be aware of."

Narrowing my eyes, I study Tam. She looks like she's done with the shenanigans, but sometimes it's hard to tell. I settle down on the plush tan couch which is every bit as soft in the right places and hard where it needs to be as the lounge chair. "Lay it on me".

"Well first, there's their ears."

6

Tam stayed for hours last night telling me what she knew of the Fae. It was pretty simple actually. There were 4 Courts, 2 Seelie and 2 Unseelie. From what she had observed there wasn't much of a practical difference between the types of Fae. In this Realm those who believed in the Fae, which weren't many outside of the Gifted Community, thought the Unseelie to be dangerous and the Seelie to be benevolent. Surprise! They both held equal disdain for the Human Realm. They both were just as likely to kill a human, not eat us though, as they were to ignore us altogether. They sincerely thought our realm and humans in general were subpar abominations. Just an all-around fun band of folks to kick it with until the Winter Solstice.

I hadn't gotten the feeling from the Prince that he felt that way about us, but then again it would have been pretty awkward for him to to let that slip then ask me to come hang out in his realm. I wondered if secretly he harbored those same feelings for us. For me?

After saying good night and promising to call her before I left the realm, I read what I could find in my collection of books. My 2-bedroom apartment was many things, but small was not one of them. I had turned my second bedroom into a library that would make any bibliophile jealous. I had everything from Shakespeare to Toni Morrison to Imhotep housed in floor to ceiling bookcases that clung to every wall. In all of that I had no more than 30 pages of text on the Fae Realm. It seemed the Fae were notoriously secretive. What could be happening in their realm that was so important that they would invite 4 outsiders in?

I closed the last book with information on the Fae feeling no closer to understanding them and their culture than I had when Tamra left. So far, I knew that they lived in what was like our feudal systems long ago. Their courts had subjects that were loyal because the courts took care of them, apparently in a way the subjects thought they could not take care of themselves. The courts protected their subjects and in return the subjects paid tribute. The whole thing sounded kind of pimpish to me, but I could well imagine how the Old People's policies made our Realm's look to others. I wasn't in much of a place to judge.

The Courts all had holidays that were associated with the cycle of the sun and harvest. The Winter Solstice Festival celebrated the longest night of the year. The Courts of Dusk and the Midnight Court held the Festival which lasted from the setting of the sun until it's rise. There was little else about the courts, not even the name of the 2 Seelie Courts was in any of my reading. Was it really wise to go into this so blind?

I waited for the Prince in the park. I was on the same bench we had been on the previous day. Wearing my dressiest fighting leathers under my leather trench, and Speedy (my curling blade) snug around my waist. I had chosen a festive red beret, matching scarf, and leather gloves. I hadn't really changed much about my looks. From all I had read and from what Tam told me the only real physical difference between us and the Fae were their point ears and their beauty. Apparently, there was no such thing as an unattractive Fae. Like humans they ran the gambit in skin color, hair textures, facial features, and the combinations thereof, but their ears were elongated and pointed at the top. I thought I looked good with the lack of information provided.

I closed my eyes, gathering my chakra and reached out to the Prince. The feel of the wind against my face, the shush shushing of people's skates against the hard-packed ice of the rink, and the peals of laughter from the children who were putting those poor elves to work

again today rushed in. Then I smelled
what I had been anticipating: his scent.

I turned my head to find him sitting
in the same spot he had taken yesterday.
He had his glamour back on.   Still
handsome, but nothing like what I had
seen in the Council's Chamber. I felt a
soft graze against the barrier to my mind
and raised an eyebrow.

"What is it that you can't say
here?" I looked around pointedly. There
was no one within earshot of us. He did
not respond.   Lowering his lids, he
allowed the grin to spread across his
face.

"Nothing.   Nothing at all." He
reached out his hand to me.

I nodded my head, preparing my
senses for the onslaught of his smell,

the heady feeling of the jaunt itself and believing (probably foolishly) that I was ready for anything. His hand was so warm it was almost hot to the touch. It reminded me of the heated towels you get when you go to a top-notch spa. Not too hot, just hot enough to feel decadent. I allowed myself to feel the decadence of him for just that moment and then we were traveling through time and space together to his realm.

7

We stopped before a large stone archway. It had to be over 30 feet high and looked as though it had been carved into the very mountain. Here it was night time and like the desserts in our realm it was cold at night. I closed my eyes to listen to the sounds of this dessert. I could feel that it was teeming with life.

The Prince began to stride up the steps of the archway and I followed. There was too much to look at, listen to, observe. I was totally unprepared for the sheer beauty, the size, and the wonder of the place. I pulled back a little from his onward press. He turned to face me, the face of the Fae Prince I had seen in the chamber. He looked impatient, slightly put out, and absolutely delicious. Even in the low light of the moon, there was a blaze dancing in his eyes. His close-cut hair so shiny in that it fought with his eyes for my attention.

I reached out for his mind, gently asking to be allowed inside. *I'm sorry. There's so much beauty to see here.* His face softened, the fire in his eyes danced, and he slowed his pace.

I allowed myself to be led up the steps and into the mountain side. The interior hallway was enormous, lit on both sides by torches at least 6 feet tall, each one about 3 feet from the other. The arched ceiling was almost reflective due to its smoothness. The polished floors were lain with what looked like fine Turkish rugs, but they were clearly not of our realm, not with that finish or that design. I longed to bend to touch the rugs to find out what material made them, but a pace didn't allow it. At the end of what I now thought of as the Great Hall, there was another flight of steps which appeared to be of the same material.

It is carved into the mountain and we are nearing its heart.

You are correct. Prince Tomas' response startled me out of my thoughts. I had been too busy sight seeing to remember to shield my mind again. That was bad form, even for a Rookie.

I hope he didn't catch that as I try to make my oversight seem intentional with more conversation. *Is your mother waiting for us?*

Tomas' grip become just a bit tighter with his reply, *My mother waits for no one.* With that I feel his mind close off to me and close mine in kind. Happy to be alone with my thoughts again,

I wonder what that was all about. I guess even princes have issues with their parents.

When we reach the interior chamber of the great hall, I have to work very hard not to gape. It is more than written words could have described. The etchings covering the majority of the walls are reminiscent of exquisite, the valleys made by the carvers are adorned with jewels of almost every color running from floor to ceiling in some places and in other places there are none at all. The pattern of the wall is both random and thought out as if it were a puzzle or perhaps a map. The room is the poshest lounge I have ever laid eyes on. The fine detail of the furniture even from 15

feet away was evident. Every seat, every
table, every area rug, and pillow looked
like it had been hand made with nothing
but pure opulence in mind.

"You finally made it." An icy female
voice greets us. If that could be called
a greeting.

Standing before a window, a female
Fae glowers at us. I know she was not
there a moment ago, but I didn't sense
her come in. I tried not appear
surprised and managed to cover my
surprise when she spoke. Or at least I
thought that I'd managed to suppress it.

"Auntie." Prince Tomas held my hand
aloft as he presented me before the
present members of the Queen's Court. I
spied 3 more on the platform now. "This
is Dyana. She has heard our request and

come nigh." His Aunt turned her full attention to me. Making not even the slightest attempt to hide the fact that she was looking me up and down.

A male Fae to the left of her cleared his throat as he stepped forward.

In my mind the clear picture of him behind Tomas' Aunt, holding her by the hair while he licked her neck appeared. The picture was gone as quickly as it had come.

"You must forgive Zorya for her rudeness. We were in the middle of something pressing when you arrived." I turned my full attention to him. "I am Set, Master at Arms."

I stared at him stupidly, trying to figure out how he had managed to show that to me. My guard was back up; he should have had to ask to enter.

"I'm sure you've heard of me." He smirked. Zorya barely tried to hold back a snarky little laugh. I tucked that one away. I'd ask Tomas about it later.

"See your little friend to her quarters", Zorya ordered. It is too late to seek an audience with the Queen. She is tending to other affairs."

"Yes, Auntie" Prince Tomas nodded his head in agreement and turned on his heels.

The picture of Set pulling Auntie Zorya's hair making her neck move first left than right as he nibbled her throat entered my mind as uninvited as the last picture and was gone just as fast.

"I am sorry to have caused an inconvenience." I stuttered at a loss for what to say as I followed Tomas back down the steps and into the Great Hall.

When I thought we were out of range, I dared to whisper to him. "What was that about Set being sure I heard him?"

Tomas smile came back full force. "You may have over done it a bit with the ears."

"Huh?" My hands flew to my ears of their own accord. "What do you mean?"

"Fae ears are larger than humans' ears. That is true, but yours are a little more...um...robust than usual."

"I'm hungry." I groused, "Where can we get a snack around this place?" I focused on fortifying the wall around my mind so no one would be privy to my next and most private thoughts. *More robust than usual, huh? Very funny, Tamra. I* *couldn't very well change them now that the Master and Mistress of Tools had made fun of them.__*

Sullenly I followed the Prince as he led me down another one of those beautifully decorated halls to my quarters. Outside of the double doors, two Fae attendants waited patiently. Both looked to be in their early 20s, both were not quite beautiful, but by no means unattractive. They were dressed in the colors of the Court of Dusk, a deep violet and a soft cornsilk yellow. Their dresses were loose and what I would imagine a peasant girl from the early times of the Old People would have worn. The material looked to be cotton or something close enough to be its cousin. The deep purplish blue of the dress was offset by cornsilk stitching and of course the aprons that they wore were of pure white. My eyes flew to their ears to do a bit of comparison and found that mine were almost 2 times as big as either of their ears. I cursed Tamra and her friggin jokes again but watched carefully as their interaction with the Prince began.

When the Prince stood in front of them, they both did a full curtsy in unison holding their skirts to the sides and bowing their heads, never making eye contact with either of us.

"Good evening, Prince Tomas." They chimed together. It was almost like a song the way it was said.

"Good evening, ladies." Tomas bent slightly at his waist giving a little salute with his right hand as he did so. I thought the attendant to the right was going to break out in giggles, but she managed to hold herself together. "This is our esteemed guest, Dyana. She is visiting our Court from our Sister Court. Please treat her as you would treat me." They murmured their agreement, unlatched the doors and shuffled to the sides to open them.

I had been so taken by the beauty of the hallways that I hadn't even thought to wonder how they were being kept so warm, but the rush of even warmer air that poured from the room made me curious how this was happening. How could a palace built into the face of a mountain be so warm?

"Please prepare yourself for a late

dinner, Dyana. The ladies will alert me when you are ready."

I was too dumbstruck to do anything other than nod. I walked into the entry room.   The two attendants already bustling about. Neonie, the younger of the 2 in my estimation and the one who no doubt was crushing big time on Tomas, began to help me out of my coat. I shooed her away as politely as possible. I didn't want to give away my weapons. I trusted the Prince, but I did not know these other people. Well, not people. How did they refer to themselves? I'll add that to my list of questions.

Fiona, the elder of the attendants, was drawing my bath water in an interior room. Neonie showed me to my sleeping quarters, quietly closing the door behind her as she left. The bed stood high and proud in the middle of the room. It was carved of an exquisite dark wood. If we had been in my realm, I would think that it was mahogany. Here I was unsure. The linens on the bed were of different textures, each looked cozier than the last. There was a giant fireplace of a marble like material that jutted out from the smooth walls. The walls in this room shone a glossy neutral as if the room had not only carved into the mountain, but then had been polished. Beautiful tapestries twice my height hung from the wall depicting scenes of the forest, the skies, and the mountains. The windows were open to the night, but there was not cold air passing through them. The motion of air in the room was from what appeared to be venting about 1/2 way up the 20 foot walls. I had never dreamed of such luxury here or anywhere. I didn't want dinner. I wanted to stay here in this room and luxuriate until I was absolutely needed.

I drew Speedy quietly. It wouldn't do to have the blade whipping around in the rooms where the only noise was the quiet bustling of attendants. A girl could get used to this. I wound the curling blade tightly and placed it in one of the drawers of an ornately carved dresser. The dresser was filled with gorgeous lingerie in almost every shade. I carefully placed my blade in the back of the 3rd drawer which was filled with satin underthings. The first drawer was filled with lace and the second drawer was filled with soft cotton things. I turned to the closet. Its wooden door had been left ajar and I could see from here that it was fully stocked with everything from fighting leathers to soft dresses for tea time. Did they do tea time here? It felt like they would. I removed a robe of deepest purple from the closet as I prepared for my bath. I could get used to this place. I could get used to it real quick.

This was more like an elaborate dream than an assignment. Bath time had been every bit as opulent as the castle itself. The water had been just the right temperature with the lightest scent of lavender. In this room and all of the other rooms I'd seen so far, the light came from torches set as sconces. The torches burned but gave off nothing other than light, there were no embers, they didn't appear to be getting smaller, and they didn't give off heat. The heat was coming from elsewhere. *Living a better life through magic.* I thought sinking down in the tub allowing the warm water to envelope me.

When I emerged from the tub, I headed to the vanity area. There are bottles and flasks and tubes of different pastel color, thick creams, thinner creams, perfumes of varying intensity, and lip glosses. They do know how to treat a guest. That was in the minuscule amount of the literature I'd been able to find, and it was true. In the bedroom there were 3 dresses laid out. All of them were modest, no plunging necklines, sequins, or flashy materials. I picked the yellow dress.

As if she had knowledge of what was going on in the room, Neonie came in as I finished dressing, gently led me to sit at the vanity, and informed me that she would be dressing my hair. I made a few attempts at conversation, after receiving the most non-committal answers I had ever heard, I decided silence was better. Neonie could have been one of the fabled politicians of the Old People. She talked but was saying nothing of substance. I wonder if it was coached for my visit or if it was the way of the attendant. Either way, it wasn't getting me anywhere.

The Prince showed up at my door just

as Neonie finished adding the last jewel to my hair. She had opted for a 1/2 up 1/2 down style. It was a mild bouffant in the front with a lot of tendrils. I thought she had been trying to hide my protruding ears, but it could be the style here. Who knew? The back was wild and curly. The way that I preferred my hair. There were small yellow and purple jewels pinned throughout the front of the style like fireflies had lit in my hair during moonlit walk.

This was all very nice, but it was also a distraction. A lovely distraction that I hoped to have more time enjoy later, but I needed to get moving on gathering intel if I was going to be of any use. To be quite honest, my two biggest suspects for chicanery were Thing 1 and Thing 2, the Master of Arms and his hot little honey. I wasn't sure what their deal was, but that little intro was weird. The million dollar was question was how had Set managed to project those images in my mind. Had anyone else seen them or had they been just for me? What a cringe worthy thought.

When I emerged from my bed chamber into the exterior sitting room, the Prince was standing alone in front of yet another giant marble fireplace. He was dressed in what looked to be a thick linen suit. The cut was impeccable showing off the broadness of his shoulders and rippling softly around his biceps. The dark color of the suit played against his skin making it look even more burnished than before. His amber eyes and ruddy hair shone in the light of the many torches and reflected he flames of the fire.

I fortified my mental wall as I took his arm. I knew there would be a sensation when I touched him, and I was not wrong. The sensation was even stronger here than it had been the first time.

He smiled down at me. "We'd better go. Auntie and Set are waiting for us."

The look of horror was real, and I didn't even bother trying to hide it.

"They want to get to know you. You know, see who we've invited into our home."

I nodded an agreement that I did not feel at all.

Set and Zorya were already seated around the round table in the surprisingly intimate dining room. The table looked big enough for at least 8, but there were only places here for 4. At least there were no surprises there. The table was dressed in ivory linen, the china gleamed, as did the gold hued cutlery. There were several serving bowls on the table as well as multiple jugs containing what looked like water and wine.

Set spoke first, "I hope you don't mind. I have dismissed the attendants. We don't require any extra ears for this." I didn't miss the little smirk that appeared on *Auntie's face, but I kept cool and simply nodded.

Tomas pulled my chair out for me. Unfortunately, I was seated next to Set not that sitting next to Auntie Z would have been any more fortunate. Set leaned close to me and sniffed. *Did this dude just sniff me?* I shot at Tomas without bothering to ask to enter his mind. I could tell by his cough that he got my message.

"You have done quite well emulating us, Dyana. Your scent is a bit off and, well," Set smiled brightly at me, "you know about your other gaffe, but overall very nice job"

"Thank you." I forced out, reaching for the wine that Tomas had just poured. I knew a bit about the Fae wine, it's unusual strength, but I needed something if I was going to be able to get through this dinner.

I felt a little nudge in my mind. It was not Tomas. It was Set. He was smiling at me a toothy grin that made me want to punch him right in the face. I lowered my wall just the slightest bit.

You've closed the back door. Very impressive. Remember there is almost always a second and sometimes 3rd point of ingress.

I pushed him back out and set up the wall again. Refortifying against him. What a creep!

The late dinner was delicious, and we ate in mostly silence after the first jab by the Set. A few just short of polite questions were thrown my way by Auntie Z. Tomas helped by fielding a couple of the easier questions about the

Human Realm. I was feeling a bit loose thanks to the wine and decided it was time that I got a few questions answered myself.

"Set, I found very little literature on this realm when researching for this *mission." Set looked marginally surprised that I addressed him. "Why is there so little info available on this realm?

"Darling, girl. Why would we give precious information to outsiders?" Zorya asked.

"Well, for starters, when you need assistance from outsiders a little background would help." Trying my best to be nonchalant, I took a sip of wine. I could absolutely feel the anger coming off of Auntie Z. She probably should have waited to be spoken to if she wasn't ready for an answer like that.

Set decided to pick up the ball, "We don't share information so that it won't be misused."

That piqued my interest and I turned to face him. "Misused how?"

"For instance, people believe that iron can kill us. This was misinformation that we planted hundreds of years ago, just to see what would happen." Set looked me in the eye and continued, "Men are still making weapons of iron and coming to try to kill us with them."

"That information is still circulating. I saw it in at least 3 of the 4 articles I read. I wonder why it hasn't been updated?"

"Because we kill them, Dyana." Auntie Z looked at me over the top of her wine glass, a faint smile on her lips. "We kill them before they have the chance to correct the disinformation. That is what we do to someone that seeks to hurt us."

Score one for Auntie Z. But she couldn't really think that I was trying to hurt anyone at this table or Fae in general. That withstanding, what an interesting piece of information about the Fae. They intentionally plant misinformation. How close was the misinformation to the truth?

Tomas cleared his throat. "Thank you for joining us for our late meal, Auntie. Set." He nodded at them both in turn standing up to assist me from my chair. "I have a big day planned for our guest tomorrow. She needs her res."

Auntie Z smiled like a predator I had no doubt she fancied herself to be, first directing her gaze at Tomas and then landing on me. "You shouldn't go to bed on a full stomach. Please let us take you for a tour of the castle. It's lovely in the moonlight."

Set rested his hand over hers, "Zorya, there is much for us to discuss and it is getting late. Perhaps Tomas can give the tour in your stead."

"Very well. My apologies for being unable to escort you." She slid her hand out from his , reaching for her wine. I met my gaze over the lip of the glass. The look told me she would still be watching whether she escorted us or not.

My look told her I hoped she liked what she saw.

The image of Set standing behind her, hands all over her, popped into my mind just briefly and without as much clarity as the images he had pushed to me before. My eyes flicked to him. He was looking at me innocently, smiling ever so slightly.

"Good night to you both and see you on the morn."

"Until then." I muttered, thankful to feel Tomas steering me out of the room and into the hall.

8

Those two were ridiculous. Between her throwing barbs for no reason and his porno picture show how was I supposed to be able to help the Fae? I was beginning to think they didn't even want help. Those 2 certainly weren't acting like it. They couldn't be a part of whatever scheme the Fae thought was underway. They were purposely being unhelpful, almost combative. No one would be that obvious. What was their deal?

I felt the soft tug of Tomas pulling me towards the left. "Where are we going?"

He smiled over his shoulder. "At last you have decided to keep me company and not be lost in your own thoughts! Shai be blessed!!"

I smiled back sheepishly. "But, seriously, dude. Where are you taking me?"

Tomas threw his head back and laughed. The same laugh the he had laughed the first day when he took me on my very first jaunt. The laugh that promised love, light, and more amusement than one could stand.

"That is the first time anyone has referred to me as a 'dude'. I think I quite like it."

"Is there an answer to my question coming any time soon?"

The only reply was more of that laughter - deep and inviting and urging me to join. I was Fae with a Fae Prince touring a palace carved into a mountain in the moonlight. My laughter joined his, the headiness began, and we were off on another jaunt.

9

We came to a rest at what seemed like the peak of the tallest mountain on what I think was the west side of the range. The view we were facing showed some desert greenery and not much else. I dared a glance straight down. The chipped face made the way down more like a cliff than a mountain side. Tomas, still holding my hand, pulled it gently turning my gaze from the precipice to what he had brought me here to see. The mountain top was no longer just a mountain top. It was a collection of pools. The pools, like everything else, were carved into the mountain. They seemed to step down one after another. I counted 8 and I was pretty sure that there were at least 2 more that were too far for me to spot from here.

"This is our reservoir - our main source of drinking water."

"It's amazing," I managed to stammer out. "How was it made?"

"Oh, you know" he shrugged, "fairy dust and all that."

I turned to look at him to see if he was serious. I didn't think so, but I didn't really know what to believe. He was smiling, the light of the moon dancing in his amber eyes, playing on his russet hair, and glossing off his burnished skin. "Are you serious?"

"Don't you trust me?" He retorted. He clutched his right hand to heart contorting his face with disbelief. "It was made with a bit of magic but mostly with the aid of the architects of the court."

I turned back to the pools, wanting to dip my fingers into the dark water and watch the ripple. "They are all connected?"

"Yes. The water is in its rawest form here on top and has been through several cleaning processes by the time it reaches the last reservoir and becomes available for the Fae of our court to drink."

"What about the Fae who are not of your court? Do they have similar set ups?"

He shook his head and shrugged his shoulders. "I've more to show you. Will you see?" He extended his right hand.

"I would see, but I would not jaunt.

Can't we just walk?"

He grinned. "How about we fly?"

Lowering his arm and rushing toward me, he took me in his arms jumping off the edge of the mountain. I wrapped my arms around his shoulders and my legs around his back in surprise just as he spread his wings. The whoosh of his wings was loud and almost frightening. I had just about written the wings off as disinformation. Where the hell had they come from? Had I not flown in so many of my other forms I probably would have fought him, but I loved the feeling of flying.

"I love your enthusiasm, but could you loosen the death clutch?"

I had been too enthralled by his wings and confused about how they were hidden so well to realize that my grip was probably going to cause us to crash. I touched his wings wanting to know all I could about them - how they worked, where they had been when I couldn't see them, what was their weight.

"Hey! You can't just touch a dude's wings." Tomas yelled over the wind.

I ignored him, feeling between his shoulders, touching where they met his back.

"Unless you want to plummet to the ground, you've really got to stop."

It was my turn to laugh - hard, carefree, and full of joy. "Then I suggest you land."

Tomas took me on a flying tour of the Court of Dusk. It turned out to be a thriving group of cities flanked on three sides by mountain ranges on the fourth by a large and somehow ominous looking body of water. The body of water didn't seem to belong in this land, not that I was any type of aficionado on what should and should not be in this realm. Yet, still, it didn't seem to belong.

When I asked Tomas about it, he told me that was a lesson for another day. I agreed to drop it for now, if he agreed to answer all my questions about his wings. This brought a fire dancing in the amber of his eyes. He smiled down at me, holding me closer than really necessary. I let him. The wind in my face, his body so close, the dreaminess of this entire experience - I didn't want any of it to stop.

"Tomorrow, Dyana. I promise."

We landed in the city center of the capital city, Petra. There were blocks of greenery surrounding by walkways leading to a tall building made of stone as exquisitely crafted as all of the buildings we had flown over and as magnificent as the entrance to the castle itself. Tomas told me that this was where his mother normally held court, where the keepers of the temples came to hold their rituals, and where tributes took place. It was in many ways the epicenter of the court far more than the palace was.

Tomas retracted his wings as we walked. I could no longer see them, but I thought I could see slits in the fabric of his top that must have allowed them to expand. Through the shirt his back looked so smooth and it was too form fitting to hide anything. So where were the wings now? I reached out and touched him again, running my palm down his chiseled shoulder toward the center of his back determined to find where those wings sprouted from. He stopped abruptly. I stopped with him, my hand lowering to where Speedy would normally be resting. Instinctively, I was on high alert.

"I didn't realize you were so forward." He said playfully. "Not that I mind."

"I'm sorry." I rushed along feeling embarrassed, "I'm just so curious. I've never seen anything like it. There's nothing in the literature -" He held up his hand. Thankfully stopping me from blathering on like an idiot.

"I know, and you will have your answers tomorrow. I promised." He took my hand in his as we faced each other under the moon of his court pressing my hand to his heavily beating heart. "Touching my wings does something to me. You know?"

If it was anything like what his hard chest and the look, he was giving me was doing to me, I knew it was time to get back to the castle and our separate rooms now. I shook my head that I understood feeling slightly chastised and wanting to continue touching just for a little bit longer.

"Was it in the literature what it's like to be with the Fae?" he waggled his eyebrows, "They say that you can never get enough once you've had a taste."

"I wonder who planted that little bit of misinformation." I snorted removing my hand from his chest and his grip with a smile.

"Ouch, you really know how to hurt a dude."

Back in my quarters, attendants had already laid out three choices of night clothes and drawn a bath which was somehow still steaming. I'm not sure how much of what I've seen is actually Fae magic and how much of it is my imagination at this point. It seems that they use magic for everything. I wonder if they tire like human mages or if their well is endless. I tucked that question away for Tomas and made for the bath.

As for the rest of what I learned this evening there wasn't all that much. I'd only met 2 members of the Court besides the Prince. His interest seemed more in having fun than it was in protecting whatever the Fae brought me here to protect. I still had absolutely no clarity about how I could actually assist this court. Auntie Z and Set were not so happy to have me here or at least not particularly welcoming. Neither of them really seemed to have very much to hide. Set certainly wanted me to know all about their sordid little affair. Auntie Z would be the perfect suspect with her blatant lack of hospitality, but villains were rarely so obvious.

In short, I saw nothing that made mc

fear that something was awry which was little comfort since I had no idea what passed for normal in the Court of Dusk. I wonder what makes the Fae think something was going to happen. Maybe it was paranoia. Whatever the case, this bath was going to be awesome.

I lay in bed reaching out to the astral realm, wondering if someone would answer me tonight. Ashka's voice would be welcome. I could do to talk to Tamra. Curse her for her shitty advice about my ears and ask her for a better advice on what I should be doing. There was no reply to my tentative hello.

I always wanted to be among the Fae. Even when I thought they were just part of some of the better tales of the old people, way before I joined the Council and found that they were actually real beings. That had been enough of a reason to take this mission, but I'm having some real second thoughts about my ability to be successful here with this little to go on.

If there was one thing I have learned in my short and sometimes unbelievably hard life, you take the good with the bad. There was still a whole hell of a lot of good here. It was truly possible I could learn to fly in a form that was close to my resting form. I could carry information back to the Council about the Fae so the next member could be prepared (unlike me). Not a bang up day, but not a bust. I could live with that. I closed my eyes, not seeking to enter the astral plane or be summoned into it and found my way to sleep.

10

In the morning, I was awakened by the sound of birds that I wasn't familiar with outside my window. I could sense more than I could hear the bustling of the attendants of the court and its members in the palace. It sounded as if today was a busy day for everyone in the castle. Winter Solstice was tomorrow days and unlike holidays back at home, the Fae decorate, celebrate, and take it down in a day's period. Today would be a day full of preparation.

I loved holidays! I didn't have

much of a family experience before I became a member of the council. I don't know if I would count that as a real family experience either, but Tamra was like an annoying older sister and Ashka a strict mother/father whatever gender Ashka was. I thought of her as a her, but she was pretty gender neutral so I wouldn't be too surprised if I was wrong there. The holidays brought out the best in most people in our realm so even without a family, there were plenty good tidings to go around. Too bad it takes a special day to make humans be humane, but I'll take it.

There was a soft knock at my door. It seems I wasn't the only one sensitive to sound in the castle. It was Neoni.

"Hello, Miss." She lowered her head

in greeting and I did the same. "We have been asked to help make preparations for the festival before breakfast this morning."

"Umm..ok." I opened the door fully letting her in. I didn't expect the four additional Fae who trooped in behind her. "Is all this necessary for breakfast?" I asked.

N turned to me, unable or guileless enough not to hide her surprise. "Miss, they are here to prepare you ensemble for the Solstice Festival."

"Yes", an older Fae stated as she raised my arms and began taking measurements, "the Prince has given us very specific instructions."

"He has?"

"Yes, Miss. He has."

I stood still at the middle of the bustle. There were measurements taken and called out, swatches of color held up against my skin and separated into what I assumed were yes, maybe, and no piles, and the most amusing was Neoni herself. She was playing with my hair, I suspect she was trying to find ways to draw less attention to my ears.

They buzzed around me and I studied them. Their outward anatomy so similar to mine. I noticed a few things that I immediately tweaked in my own appearance. Their finger nails had a different sheen to them than my normal nails, their hair was fabulously healthy and shiny looking, and their skin was incredibly clear almost without pores. It was like they were all in the same collagen supplement commercial.

I tried to catch their scent since Set had been so kind as to point out that mine was off, but I couldn't put my finger on the difference. To be honest, I had never thought to adjust my scent separately when I shifted. It wasn't a normal requirement when shifting, but the added layer of realism would only help. I wonder how Set would sleep with the knowledge that he inadvertently helped me. Not well, I hoped.

The most important thing about their anatomy and what would ultimately make me a true Fae when I shifted was an understanding of how their chakra, their life energy, ran through their bodies. I closed my eyes, blocking out the chattering and the soft noises of their work. Seeing with my mind, I had a clear view of their energetic bodies. Their chakra ran through the normal points, the same as other living creatures, but its level was much more intense and the flow was unique. Instead of traveling in straight, thin, and determined lines, their flow was more like a tumultuous river. The energy chased itself around the path in steady waves, much thicker than even the most powerful mage I'd encountered, seeming to lap at the surrounding tissue. The surrounding tissue also interacted with the chakra differently, pulsing around the chakra flow. *Interesting.*

I turn my attention to their heart, lungs, and other organs. They are almost exactly like ours. The lungs seem a little larger and the heart is a bit different too. I think they may have a higher flow of oxygen in their blood than we do. I wonder if the healers will have that information documented. After breakfast, I would insist on going to the library, even if just for a couple of hours. This part of recognizance was as important, at least to me, as the filling out of my knowledge about what the hell I was looking for in the first place.

The buzzing died down after about 1/2 an hour or so and no one seemed to notice the changes that I was making incrementally to my form. There were no clocks in this room. In fact, I don't recall seeing any throughout the castle or in the streets of the land of the Court of Dusk last night. I made a mental note to ask Tomas about it.

"Miss?"

I looked at Neomi, both eyebrows up in question.

"Breakfast will be served in 30 minutes in the Inner Court's Dining Room. I will be back in 15 minutes to do your hair." She stated matter of factly.

I guess doing my own hair was out of the question. That was fine by me. I smiled and nodded my understanding, turning to go back into my bedroom.

"The Prince has chosen an appropriate outfit for your day. It is already laid out in your room."

"He thinks of everything. Doesn't he?" I questioned with a smile.

"Yes, Miss. That is our way."

11

Breakfast had turned out to be in the same dining area where we had our late dinner last night. Thankfully Auntie Z wasn't there. Unfortunately, Set was present and accounted for. He sniffed the air when I walked in, allowed the corners of his lips to turn up in a smug and hateful little smile, and nodded my way. I was pleased to see that there were 3 other Fae joining us for breakfast. I wondered what information I could get off them.

Tomas helped me get seated next to a female Fae dressed in shimmering lavender from head toe. Her hair was so light that it was more silver than blond. She wore it swept up and adorned with pearls and what looked like sapphires. It must have taken someone over an hour to do that. It was amazing, but who had that type of time for hair? She was introduced as Freyja, Mistress of the Craft and overseer of the Festival. She cordially welcomed me, but there was a bit of wariness in her eyes as we exchanged pleasantries. Was it me that was making her wary or the lecherous way Set was peering at her over his plate? I checked the shield on my thoughts. I wasn't up for any of his XXX projections.

On Tomas's other side sat a fierce looking female Fae dressed in fighting leathers. Her leathers were shiny black and looked butter soft. The stitching on the bodice was different shades of red. It ran vertical through the entire bodice. The epaulets over her shoulders were cut to ruffle and rested prettily on her muscular arms. Her dark brown hair was pulled back into a severe bun and was adorned simply with a few red jewels. I looked at her and longed to train. I normally trained every day and seeing someone so quietly powerful made me want it. I could only imagine what training would be like in my enhanced body. *Training, is definitely going on my list right behind the library.* Tomas introduced her as Inanna.

Next to Set was another Fae male. He was dressed in a suit similar to that of the Tomas and Set. It was of the same heavy linen, midnight blue, and close cut. He was also similar in size to the Prince, but there the similarities ended.

His skin was not the sun kissed bronze of Tomas, it was decidedly pale in deference to almost everyone I had seen since I had been here. An emissary then? He was simply introduced as Merrick. No title was given. He nodded curtly when Tomas introduced us, immediately returning to his conversation with Set. I cut my eyes at Tomas. He gave an almost imperceptible shrug and began helping himself to the platter of eggs in front of him.

I had so many questions for Tomas but didn't want to let my psyche open to ask them now. I couldn't risk anyone getting in. The front door, the back door, and the side door needed to be locked up tight from here on out. I hoped I would have enough alone time with Tomas today so I could get answers.

I decided that I may as well enjoy my breakfast, observe as much as I could, and mix in with the Fae that were here. Only 2 of the 5 Fae here knew for sure that I was a human and I needed to make sure that the other 3 were not able to guess. Funny thing is Fae small talk is a lot like human small talk. I kept my answers brief and silly and them turned the question right back around on whoever asked me. I was pretty good if I do say so myself. I even pulled a chuckle out of Set that wasn't quite at my expense.

Inanna and Freyja excused themselves when their plates were empty. Set left only a few minutes after them leaning over and whispering, "I see you've improved yourself. Even your scent has improved." I didn't turn my head to look at him, but I did smile. That is until he added, "But you probably heard me thinking that." He chuckled, nodded to the Prince who was looking a bit too amused, and sauntered out of the room.

When I looked at Tomas, he shrugged and grinned, "It was funny."

I guess it was a little funny, but still.

"Let's get out of here. I have much to show you today. There are things you should know before the Festival begins."

That was an understatement.

12

Tomas led me back to my quarters, leaving me to freshen up. The delicate dress I had chosen for breakfast wasn't suitable for what was planned today and that was fine by me. Although I felt like a beautiful princess in the clothes, I wasn't here to be a beautiful princess. I had business to attend to and doubted that these gorgeous and surprisingly comfortable slippers were the right choice for my work.

I had insisted on taking a glass of what I thought was the sweetest and freshest orange juice I had ever had with me and was delighted to see there was a pitcher on the table in the waiting room. *Now when did he have time to do that?* I thought.

The best surprise came when I walked into the bedroom. There on the bed were three suits of exquisite fighting leathers, similar in style to the one that Inanna wore at breakfast. I hadn't bothered to look at them last night. Who would have though fighting leathers could be so alluring? I could barely contain myself, I almost squealed with glee when I touched them. The interior was so soft in direct contrast to the exterior which was alarmingly hard. *How could this be?* My reinforced leathers that I had worn here didn't offer even half of the protection these would.

Where was Neoni when you needed her. This morning dress, although beautiful, was going to be a project to get off alone. I considered partially shifting but didn't want to risk even a small signature of magic use. *How would I sound explaining that I had to shift to get out of my clothes?*

"I can help you with that." A familiar male voice said from behind me.

Behind me? I hadn't heard anyone come in. I whipped around and there he was. Set sat in the parlor sipping from my glass of orange juice. I was so angry that I knew better than to speak. I imagined slapping the glass out of his hand letting the sweet juice slosh onto that impeccable suit maybe get a couple of pieces of glass stuck in his hair. That soothed me a little bit and I waited. I knew from training the first one to talk in these situations loses the advantage. I would sit here all day until he talked first. Whatever little game he was playing, I would not give him the upper hand. Well, I wouldn't give him the upper hand any more than he already had it.

I walked over to the table and calmly sat down taking what I hoped was a casual pose. Crossing my left leg slowly over my right and hooking my right arm over the back of my chair, I tilted my head to the right and cocked an eyebrow. *What?* my gesture asked.

I felt him grazing softly against my mental protections asking to be let in. This was a surprising change of events. Surely, he could have gotten in when I thought I was alone. Had he been in there when I was alone. I hadn't felt him, but that didn't necessarily mean he hadn't been there. I had read that some of the Fae are masters of the shadow. They were able to appear anywhere that shadows fell. Was he one of those masters? I gave him a bright smile and tugged on my left ear? *We'll be speaking in here, buddy*, the gesture said. *Can't wait to hear what you have to say.*

He put on an exasperated but amused face. He really was handsome. The literature had not lied about the beauty of the Fae. As much as I wanted to smash Set's face in, I had to admit that I could look into sage green eyes like that all day. He pushed a little harder this time and gave a little shrug of his shoulders. This request to enter felt more like a threat than a request.

I put my bright smile back on and shrugged my shoulders right back at him, letting my head loll casually from the right to the left. *Try me,* I dared.

He laughed. "I could learn to like you."

"Be still my heart."

"Are you not concerned that Tomas will be back soon."

"Are you?"

Set took another sip of my orange juice. I thought about sending him the visual of my dumping the pitcher on his head but decided against it. Sending the thought might leave me open if I was not already.

"You are an interesting creature," he began. "I have been to your realm many times and have met others with your..." he searched for the word, "..abilities. They would never swear allegiance to anyone. They were too powerful by their own estimation. Why did you?"

"This is what you broke into my room for? To get to know me? I'm flattered." I poured myself a glass of juice. Setting the pitcher down carefully then stopping to sniff the glass before I drank. The Fae senses were very powerful and I would be able to pick up some poisons in this form, but not all. It was more of a show to let him know I didn't trust him than an act of self preservation. Who would be bold enough to try to kill me in my room in the palace not knowing when Tomas would be back? He had been bold enough to slip in here not knowing when Tomas would come back, but being caught with me alive and annoyed was very different from being caught with me dead.

"I didn't break in. The door

unlocked."

"Semantics." I dismissed his
rebuttal with a wave of my hand still
sipping at my juice. <u>What other little
tricks do you have up your sleeve?</u> I
thought, but did not send.

"Dyana, please answer my question."

The please startled me, and I
answered. "The Council offered me
stability and a place where I could
flourish."

"And have you? Flourished?"

I gestured grandly at myself,
smiling my 100 watt smile again.

"That is all? You wanted to," he
paused dramatically raising both
eyebrows incredulously, "flourish and
needed stability?"

"What exactly did you think was

going to happen when you barged or rather sneaked into my room to ask me personal questions? Huh? Did you think I would be excited that you were interested in me?" He was starting to piss me off and I really wanted to try on those fighting leathers.   I rose from my seat and gestured at the door. "Show yourself out."

"I know a lot about your kind." He said coldly. "Humans are destructive, impulsive, an all around mess. Look how the Old Ones nearly destroyed your entire realm, yet your kind has not totally abandoned their ways."

I glared at him, "Please continue."

"Gladly. I did not want anyone from your realm here - for any reason, certainly not to protect anything of value. Your kind have repeatedly shown you know nothing of what is valuable and even less about protecting what is of real value. Humans think only of enriching themselves at any cost."

"Are you finished now?"

"No. Thank you for asking. I wondered why there was such a lobby to have the Council assist us. Why did the Prince push the Queen for you? Did you wonder, Dy?"

I was annoyed that he called me by a nickname, but I could understand his line of questions. "I am the only OmniShifter blood sworn to the Inter Realm Council. I am the only one who can walk among Fae as one of them and be held accountable to Inter Realm tenets." The answer sounded weak even to my own ears.

"I see. Let's talk about the Council. Did you wonder why they gave you so little information?"

"Fae do not allow information to remain in or realm. You said as much yourself."

"You think the Council has not amassed information? Information they could have shared."

I did not reply. I wasn't sure how to reply and I didn't like what he was implying. "So, then... You can't show yourself out? Do you need my help with that?"

He sniffed, "We will talk again."

"Can't wait".

Set paused at the door, "Enjoy your new leathers. Maybe you can wear that interesting belt with them." He closed the door quietly behind him.

So he knows about my curling blade, I thought, *and wants me to know it. Why?* It didn't really matter why he wanted me to know, but I was still curious. I was pretty clear on where Set stood with me and my presence, so what was this little visit really about?

13

I decided not to tell Tomas about the unpleasant visit. I had a lot I want to cover today, and I don't want to waste time on Set and his little games. Tomas was unexpectedly agreeable to both my request to go to the library and my request to train. The only caveat was that there would be a time limit to the library that he would set, and he was able to choose the type of training. I agreed to both.

Tomas explained the library was one of many throughout the cities that comprised the Court of Dusk, but it was the only one that was private. Housed in three enormous connected rooms in the castle, the private library called, The Library of the Court, was straight out of my dreams. I've loved to read and even to study since I was a little girl. Finding out information I hadn't even known I was curious about, living vicariously through the experiences of others written on the page, and playing both sides of the a philosophical argument are all things I considered magical and the library was where the most of that type of magic lived.

I could almost feel that magic thrumming throughout the rooms. There were beautiful casks with large scrolls sticking out of the tops throughout the library, quill pens and loose paper on each fine wood table scattered throughout the room just waiting for a visitor to scribble down a note, and plush seating areas perfect for hours of lounging. The light was bright and welcoming. Those strange torches which burned bright while producing no ash cast light down from the chandeliers which hung from the high ceilings. They were stationed along the brightly shining wall made of the mountain themselves. It was so picturesque; it was almost easier to believe that I was reading a book about walking the rooms of an exquisite library with a handsome Fae Prince than to believe this was a reality. *But it is,* I said to myself, *and I have a job to do.*

Tomas leads me to one of the exquisite desks. I can't help but to run my hands across wood of the chairs, the fine craftsmanship making the simple curves of the chair eye catching, but I cut it short. I've only got 1 full day before the night of the festival and I have no more of an idea about what I'm looking for than when I got here.

"Begin with this book." He said as a finely bound book appeared out of thin air in front of where I sat. He paced a few steps from me and continued, "Don't get too bogged down with that text. Most of what you will need to know, I will show you later."

"Will you tell me more about why I'm here?"

"You are here to observe and report."

"Observe what?" Tomas looked at me and said nothing. His face saying that I should be clear on all of this.

"You are going to have to give me more to go on." I pushed.

Tomas turned from me, walking towards a wall full of books. I felt a soft nudge at my mind. I opened it for him, closing the door once he entered.

You are supposed to observe without forming any opinions. That is why I asked for an outsider.

You asked for an outsider or you

asked for me?

Both.

What is the big secret?

I cannot tell you, but I can show you something.

I hope that's enough. I shot back at him. Softly, but firmly pushing him out of my head and locking my mind away from him. Turning my attention back to the book in front of me. This whole hush hush thing was beyond old. I had been so excited to come here, to be requested by name, that I hadn't fully vetted this before accepting. I hoped I wouldn't regret it, but I was starting to be pretty sure that I would.

"You have until the sands run out and then we're off to training." Tomas interrupted my thoughts making me jump just a little.

An hourglass appeared on the table in front of me. The sounds of its sands sliding through the small opening between the top and the bottom was a little distracting, but I'd concentrated in far more difficult situations than this. The Fae senses were truly amazing. Even the smell of the paper and the feel of the book were enhanced thanks to the upgrades I was making to my form this morning. I held the book to my face breathing in deeply, a little book lover ritual I have.

"If you're not going to take study time seriously, we can just head straight to training." Tomas teased.

I stuck my tongue out at him and crossed my eyes. Turning back to my book, I could hear his lips pulling back from his teeth in a smile. Another book materialized in front of me. Its pages flipping to a stop about halfway through. "Show off!" I muttered.

"Read that chapter too." He said cheerily, his steps growing fainter as he headed for the door behind me. "I'll be back soon."

I muttered a goodbye and peeked at the other book. *Hmmm.... the astral plane.* I smiled in appreciation. *Today is going to be interesting.*

14

True to his word, Tomas had appeared just as the last sands settled on the bottom of the hourglass. I had read a synopsis about the Fae anatomy, including their wings, and the chapter on the astral plane. I heard his approach and was waiting for him at the door. My form was even more enhanced than when he had left me earlier. He smiled and nodded his head.

I had been thinking about the Fae anatomy the wrong way, approaching it as I would someone of my realm. Fae are different. In this form, not only were my senses heightened, but the flow of chakra through my body was also enhanced. All of the magical things I saw through the cities of the Court and especially in the castle were controlled by chakra infusion. Fae infused a bit of themselves into an object and the object behaved as they would have it. This was a normal way of life for them. This everyday magic was innate, not even practiced. It was fascinating. The flow of my chakra now imitated that of the common castes of Fae. They had the everyday magic abilities, but could not control elements, perform spells, that sort of thing. I'd need some time to work up to the chakra flow that ran through the veins of the higher castes and royalty. Their chakra flow was intimidating to say the least. I wasn't sure that I could loosen my control so much without losing it.

"Now that you see what I can do with some information, I hope that you are inspired to give me more."

"You don't let up. That's good." Taking my hand, Tomas led me from the doorway of the 2nd room of the library and into the hall.

I'm pretty sure that he's flirting with me again and I want to flirt back. I need to be focused, but a girl's got to have fun too. "So, what's next for today?" I ask in my very best professional tone.

"It's a surprise." Tomas smiled devilishly, "Rather, it's a series of surprises. That is if you are up for it."

"I'm up for anything." I answered. I wanted to take it back as soon as I said it. Hoping that my new clearer Fae complexion wasn't flushed and showing my embarrassment.

"And so am I."

"No jaunts this soon after

breakfast." I warned.

He looked at me reproachfully. "I wouldn't dream of it."

The headiness was coming back and the scent of him filled my nostrils, but it wasn't a jaunt this time. We weren't walking worlds.   It was just the closeness of him.

15

When I saw the lake my first night in the Fae Realm. My first thought was that it didn't belong there, and I wasn't that far from the truth. The lake wasn't really a lake. It was a portal, Tomas told me as we approached from above. The portal was the only door to the Fae Realm that could not be closed. There was an

Anubis in every court of the Fae. The story of their creation was lost, but all knew how to use it. The Anubis would take anyone who was able to cross the area of protection wherever they desired. They need only speak their destination.

"Interesting." I said thoughtfully. "What language do you need to use?"

Tomas looked utterly confused. "What language?"

I widened my eyes at him and shook my head quickly. The universal gesture for "duh".

"Dyana, there is only one language."

"Here?"

"Everywhere. Every when." He splayed his hands out in front of him as if he were a magician doing his big reveal, "Same language."

"That's not possible."

"But it is. Those who live in your realm have created differences where there are none. The differences are so far embedded you no longer recognize the sameness."

"Is this going to be another one of those riveting humans are beneath us conversations?" I rolled my eyes.

"Another one?"

I ignored his question, not wanting to talk about my time with Set this morning. "So, what are we doing here today?"

"This is your first lesson. Do you see what is below?"

I thought about calling the sight of the falcon, before realizing that my Fae eyes could do the job. I narrowed them and focused on the desert in front of the shimmering Anubis that I had mistaken for a body of water. There were multiple lion-like cats prowling the area, partially hidden by the shrubbery. I nodded my head.

"Those are the Hell Catts. They are the protectors of the portal. Only the Royal Families of the 4 courts are able to cross into this area without being torn to shreds."

"What is the lesson here?" I was beginning to feel very nervous. We were losing height and getting closer and closer to the ground. The Hell Cats were raising their heads, long blond tails ticking back and forth slowly, as we descended.

"What do you think?" Tomas said

playfully.

Clearly, he was ignoring my growing fear. I was damn near horrified by this point. I could smell the heat coming off of the ground as well as I could smell the pheromones of the Hell Cats. Their attentions were turning to us. I could feel the intensity of their stares narrowing from looking at us to looking at just me. I grabbed onto Tomas tighter as I felt his grip loosening. My feet were merely feet from the ground at this point.

The Hell Cats were watching me intently. One of the four that I could see, I could smell 3 more, was rising from its lounging position behind a patch of thorny looking shrubs. Its eyes glittered in the sunlight. I met its gaze. The bright red of the eyes was unnerving, but I knew if I looked away, I have lost. I steady my breathing. *I will not embarrass myself before Tomas. I will not fail the council. I will not fail myself.*

My feet brush the ground then flatten bringing an abrupt end to the pep talk that I was giving myself. I remove my arms from around Tomas' neck, never breaking eye contact with the Hell Cat. I can hear the hushed sounds of 2 more approaching, one to our immediate left and one just behind us. They are no more than 25 feet away and I do not know how quickly they move.

Tomas is no longer next to me. I don't know when he moved. I don't know that it makes a difference. There are now 6 cats on the move, slowly approaching me. They are ignoring Tomas altogether.

Think, you don't have much time, I command myself. The demand seems to work as I begin going through my morning lessons. I cannot become a Hell Cat. If they are like a lion's pride, they would know I was not one of their own. At worst they would kill me for being an outsider at best they would only injure me. I couldn't afford either.

I visualize the flow of my chakra, steadying my breath, willing the flow to speed, letting go of the constraints. I push the chakra to the limit, allowing it to spill over the points, allowing it to lap at the cells around it almost haphazardly. I can feel the confusion of the Hell Cats. The one closest to me only 10 feet away, well within striking distance.

I can feel the chakra rising in my body. My heart is beating faster to sustain the increase in energy, my breathing is both deeper and faster, and my life's force is so free that I think it's going to break out of my body. I know I can't stop now, and I push it even further. The flow of the chakra getting faster. In my mind's eye, I see the energy coursing through my body. It's like a prism - all the colors of the rainbow cavorting in my energy. The pushing is over, and it is time to relax into the energy to assume it as mine. And I do.

The Hell Cat has closed the distance

between us, stalking towards me with its head down, and it's tail flat. I hold out my hand to it, open and palm up. It nuzzles my hand, licks a sandpaper tongue across my palm and walks on.

Tomas is next to me again. The light is dancing in his eyes, his wide mouth open in laughter. Before I can think better of it, I am in his arms. Running my fingers across his tight curls, pushing his head down so that his lips can meet mine, I begin kissing him. He doesn't stop me. He opens his mouth to my searching tongue, allowing my soft pants to mix with his breaths. His hands slip into my long black curls, using my ponytail to angle my head for his exploratory kisses.

I can hear the Hell Cats returning

to their late morning lounge around us. And something else. There's something else here.

I pull away from Tomas abruptly. Looking around us to see who or what has entered the area. "Do you feel that?" I ask.

"Yes" Tomas pulls me close, leaning in to pick up where we left off.

"Something isn't right." I push his hands away. I can't think with him so close. "Please, take me somewhere else?" I ask.

"As you wish," he says tucking me into his arms. The sand shudders under his feet as he takes off.

We fly without words towards Petra, the city at the center of the Court of Dusk. I begin slowly allowing the chakra to mellow it's course - taking myself from the royal caste, past the higher castes and down to the common caste again. *Everybody doesn't need to know that I'm capable of that.* I broadcast to Tomas. I'm still feeling so connected to him that I don't think to ask permission first.

You're right about that. He answers.

You heard me?

Yes, maybe tomorrow I'll tell you what that means.

Tomorrow. Always a waiting period with this one. I think to myself only this time after redoubling my mental shields. I need to concentrate on regulating my chakra. Concentration is almost impossible when I can feel the muscles in Tomas' chest working, his upper back tensing and releasing under my fingers, my nose filled with the smell of him. *I'm not here for this.* I remind myself. *But maybe I could be here for this too.* The little traitorous thought sneaks into my mind. I'm going to blame it on the chakra flow. I'm going to blame the whole incident on the chakra flow. Better yet, we will not speak of it again and we will walk to our next destination.

He brought us back to the palace. He left me at my room like a perfect gentleman after letting me know that he would be back for lunch. We would be dining in my sitting room. I had searched his face when he made the announcement, looking for a devilish little smile. There was none. I agreed and he had left.

When I entered the room, I realized I was utterly exhausted and a little gross. Flying was dusty work even when you aren't the one flapping wings. The orange juice from this morning was still on the table, condensation dripping down the side. Of course, it was. What good home wouldn't have a carafe that kept things cold. Shai and all her fates bless the Fae for their ingenious uses of magic.

After my bath, I snuggled in the comfiest robe ever and lay on my bed leisurely flipping through books Tomas must have had sent to my room. There was a history of the Fae where I found a description of the 2 types of Fae, Seelie and Unseelie. I was relieved to see this, because it would save me the embarrassment of asking. How ridiculous would be blurting out "Aren't you one of the bad Fae" after my tongue had been down Tomas' throat.

The Fae's description of themselves had nothing to do with good or bad like the literature of the Old People's said. It had everything to do with the affinity of the Courts. The Courts of the Seelie were associated with day and the Courts of the UnSeelie were associated with night. That was it. Tam had been on the up and up about that one. The book went on to describe the Courts in great detail. I thumbed through the pages quickly, I didn't think there was time for that type of study.

An hourglass appeared on my nightstand as did a note. **Lunch will arrive shortly.** I wasn't sure how I felt about this ability to just send things into my personal space. I wondered if I could do it to. Probably. I was certain that I could do it in my royal caste state, but I wouldn't risk playing games with chakra in the palace. Altering my state at the edge of the Court of Dusk in front of Hell Cats who would never breathe a word was one thing. Playing at being royal in the heart of the palace was a totally different thing.

There was a knock on the door to my rooms that was almost in time with the last drop of sand through the hourglass. Neomi and Fiona came in first ushering me to the bedroom and offering to help me get dressed. They closed the double doors between the bedroom and sitting room as four male Fae came into the parlor and began adjusting furniture. I accepted their help and used the time to study them more closely. The anatomy lesson I had earlier had not made mention of wings and I was still incredibly curious about where they were hidden.

They flitted around me. Fiona tying my corseted blouse, Neomi working on my drying hair, trying her best to get out the tangles without pulling too hard. She worked my long black curls into a tight ponytail adorned with a few pastel colored jewels. She worked her fingers on the tips of my still too big ears, fussing with them as if she would find a way to beautify them too. I giggled at the look of frustration on her face.

"Does that tickle, Miss?"

I assured her that it did not tickle, and she moved on from primping them with a small sigh and a pat that told me she had given up on them. Fiona straightened my flowing pants making sure that the corset fell over them perfectly, not a wrinkle was in sight. I surveyed their work in the mirror. My skin had taken on a sheen that mirrored theirs and my body muscled in my resting form was a sight to behold in my Fae form. My arms were sculpted, yet soft under the loose sleeves. My body looked as lithe and nimble as it felt in the near translucent ensemble.

"Let me guess. The Prince picked this out."

Neomi and Fiona lowered their faces, but not before I noticed their smiles. They retired from my room noting that the Prince would be there momentarily, and our lunch would be set out before us. They would be just a ring away if we needed them.

Tomas and I talked amicably as Neomi and Fiona swept in and out making sure our needs were met. Tomas looked refreshed in a white shirt and dark blue pants made of the same thick linen he'd worn earlier. The shirt was cut to perfection rippling across his muscled chest as he reached for his water glass. I knew he was watching me. I should have pretended not to be watching. I didn't.

A note popped up next to my glass. **Dismiss them** was written in red. I choked on the salad I had been eating. The note disappeared as Neomi rushed in to make sure everything was okay.

"I am fine. Thank you for checking and for being so close." I gave a little smile to Tomas. He rolled his eyes in response.

I felt him softly stroking at my mind, asking for entry. I shook my head, closing my eyes. If I looked at him, I would let him in. I would dismiss them. We would be in my bed.

"Yes". I heard him say.

My eyes flickered open in question.

"Yes." He said again.

"Where to after lunch?" I asked. We needed to get out of here and into the fresh air.

It was his turn to close his eyes. I felt him inviting me to his inner thoughts and followed. There we were. In my bed. He was sitting on the edge of the bed with his shirt unbuttoned, my hand trailed down his chest. Suddenly he turned me around, his fingers working quickly to untie my corset then lightly touching the exposed skin of my back.

I lingered there with him a moment longer, long enough to watch the blouse fall away from my breasts, then I left him alone in his thoughts. *Naughty, nasty prince.* I sent out to him.

You don't know the half.

Maybe I didn't, but I would like to

know. I would like it very well.

Because I had just barely made it
through lunch without dismissing Fiona
and Neomi, I insisted that I take my
leave of the Prince so that I could get
a feel for the cities by myself. I told
him that it was unlikely that the city
Fae were acting normally in his presence.
I needed to get a gauge for the baseline
of his subjects if I was going to be any
help at all. Truthfully, I needed to
get some space between the two of us. I
couldn't concentrate on anything except
the absence of his mouth on mine while he
was talking, and I was starting to think
that just might be okay.

At the center of each of the Court
of Dusk's cities was a huge park. Each

with numerous walkways within a green area that all led to a Meeting Place in the center. The Meeting Place was visited by a rotation of Court officers weekly who kept the peace, listened to the concerns of the folk, and shared any messages from the Courts. The Meeting Place at beautifully manicured oasis at the center of Petra would e he epicenter of the Festival. Tomas reluctantly agreed to take me there.

The Fae below were little more than busily moving dots at this distance. When we got to the center, I told him to drop me. The appreciation in his eyes when his arms fell to his sides and he watched me plummet towards the ground sparked something in me that I shoved away immediately. I concentrated on bending my body to the shape of the Morning Bird that I had heard when I awoke this morning. Spreading my metallic silver wings, I coasted towards the activity below.

The air rushed at my face; my wings folded back in my dive. As I approached, I could see the streets were full of Fae arranging and rearranging decorations both with magic and by hand. The decorations were shades of dusk - ranging from bright to dark and deep purples, oranges, blues, and reds. There were pops of gold and twinkling of silver thrown into the mix adding to the feel of a night sky providing the starlight and moonlight that cavort only in the night.

My pre-lunch studies said that this was one of many Fae Holidays but it was the most important holiday here in the Court of Dusk where the Royals of the Court controlled the magic of the night. Tonight would be the longest night of the year and the members of the Court and the folks of its land would bask in revelry all night. There would be drinks, dancing, laughter, and gifts.

Nestled in one of the parks trees, I heard and felt nothing but anticipation and happiness. The Land of the Court of Dusk made in the heart of mountains was a wonder to experience. I marveled at the huge trees and mature greenery. The park was so like a park in my realm, yet the climate here did not seem to support it. The air nearly crackled with life energy. The Fae's chakra was a part of everything here, even the inanimate objects pulsed

with it. How had I not felt this as soon
as I arrived?

I had seen enough. Now it was time
for Tomas to talk to me and tell me what
I was missing. Nothing in what I had
observed today would give anyone pause.
I reached out for Tomas' mind. I could
barely feel him, but knew he was nearby.
He was almost totally shut off from me.
When I reached towards him, I could only
hardly make out what he was seeing. He
was holding something in both of his
hands. It was emitting a low and steady
light from its center. I couldn't make
out what it was. His hands were covering
most of it. He seemed to be so
enthralled with the object that he didn't
sense me. I searched his mind for what
it was, trying hard not to alert him to

my presence.

I pulled the name from his mind. It is one of the 7 Hallows. Whatever that meant. I pulled back from his mind slowly, then asked for entry. I imagined more than actually felt Tomas trying to pull himself together before letting me in.

Meet me. I sent. Snapping off our connection before any of my other thoughts could become clear.

Our walk through the city's center was leisurely, the type of walk that I would have taken back home in New Delphia. It didn't seem that we were headed anywhere in particular, just 2 folks enjoying each other's company. Tomas was funny, surprisingly so. I guess

I had always thought that a Prince would be stuffy and snotty. He was the opposite and as we walked the streets of his capital city, it was clear that his subjects loved him. They came towards him without hesitation, offering their respects and refreshments. Tomas greeted them all warmly, introduced me as his esteemed guest, and moved on politely noshing fruit and sipping drinks that we were given.

What is the Hollow, I sent to Tomas hoping to catch him off guard? It doesn't work. He doesn't even break stride.

I will show you.

The Meeting Place, a simple name for such an impressive structure, began to take shape in front of us. It had the columns that I had come to expect in each building that I saw and the simple, perfect curves that were a hallmark of their architecture. *Something is here.* I thought. The thought was visceral dragging me from my leisurely walk and putting me on high alert. Resting my hand on Speedy, I stole a glance at Tomas, he was walking along as before. *Does he not feel that?*

"We are going to need to jaunt. Has your lunch settled?"

He was giving me the same annoyingly sexy smirk he had given me when he landed after I had mauled him by the Anubis. I needed him to explain to me what I saw before. I reach my hand towards him and watch the smirk turn into a grin.

Mid-step I feel the queasiness and

know that it has begun. *Can all Fae travel this way? Can I travel this way by myself now?*

I feel the soft rap at my mind's gate and allow him entry.

We are beneath The Meeting Place. I am taking you to what you have been feeling.

My eyes widened. *Does everyone feel it?*

No.

That's it. No more information? Just a simple no. *Why not?* I asked exasperated that even now getting information was like pulling teeth.

If everyone could feel it, it would not be hidden. You feel it because you are royal.

Well, that wasn't quite true, but I

hadn't started feeling it until I had loosed the royal chakra flow. Maybe that's what he meant.

Is this the artifact you were talking about? Is that what you're finally going to show me?

It is a Hallow. The first of seven.

The first of seven what?

Tomas is silent for a long while. His mind closed to me again. I wait, trying to be patient. I needed this information.

Finally, I hear him in my head. *The first of seven needed to release the Scourge.*

I grab his arm, ignoring the tingle the touch causes me. Needing him to face me and explain this. All of this. *The Scourge is a myth.*

What man cannot explain it turns to myth, but there is truth in every tale.

Tell me.

You already know.

The Scourge is an ancient tale. One that survived the destruction of the Old People. It is the tale of a ruler that will harness the power of the Demon Realm using it to unite all of the known Realms under her rule. The stories of the war are horrific. Whole realms left little more than wastelands when they dare defy her.

Why is it here? I ask him.

You already know that too.

I look into his eyes, the amber lights still dancing, debating whether to punch him or kiss him. *I do NOT know.*

There are 4 hallows in the realm of

the Fae, 2 in the realm of the Seraphim, 1 lost by the Old People in my own realm. *That is a myth.* I repeat. *Men do not know of a Realm of the Seraphim.*

Tomas' right hand tilted my head up to meet his eyes again. *The Realm of Men knows the Seraphim and the Demon Realm and many others.*

I shake my head free of his hand. He cups my face with both of his hands, guiding my eyes to his once again. *That is the true story of the Old People. That is how your realm was almost destroyed.*

Images began appearing in my thoughts of the winged Seraphim of fables and the Demon World Walkers in my realm. But this version of it was the before image with trees that were thousands of years old instead of under one hundred, mountain ranges that were not man made, natural wonders that still existed. I let the images wash over me, trying to understand what I was seeing.

"Why am I here?", I whispered.

"We are destined to save our realms."

What?

You must allow me to pause the memory of this conversation, Dyana?

Say what now?

You must allow me to pause this memory, Dyana. You cannot have this knowledge and perform your duties tonight. Our bond is too strong. I could not hide the truth from you.

You were trying to hide the truth from me? What are you even saying?

"Sleep", Tomas said quietly as if in prayer, "and forget."

16

The jaunt ended with me feeling a bit groggy this time. Maybe something I'd eaten on our walk hadn't agreed with me, but I wanted to shake the feeling immediately. Tomas had taken me from the park of Petra to the Royal Baths, a series of heated baths in what I think is the east part of the palace. I can't seem to get my bearings straight. It didn't stop me from seeing how glorious they were. Inside the heart of a mountain, like the rest of the palace, the baths were private rooms with large tubs of heated water in their center.

The tubs were bordering on the size of small swimming pools at no less than 8 x 8 feet. There was an area with cushioned seating and long coffee table filled with carafes of what looked like water and wine, cups and glasses, fruit and breads to our right. Fluffy towels and robes hung on hooks along the long wall to the left of the entry. The doors slid closed behind us as we entered our own private room.

"Isn't it illicit for the Prince to bring visitors to the baths?" I teased.

"Fishing for information?" He gave as well as he got.

"This is amazing. Fae Magic?"

"It's a hypocaust system. It was used in your realm at one time."

I turned from the spectacle that was

the room towards him wanting to see his face to see if he was still teasing. He was stripped down to his very tight white shorts. His broad chest leads down to abs that longed to be touched. I tried my best not to gape like a randy teenager, but I'd never seen a body so beautiful before. His legs were lean and muscled, the tops of the thighs lightly kissing together as they rose to where they met I forced myself to draw my eyes away from his body and to his face. It was a real struggle.

I didn't bother trying to hide what I was thinking. It would have been a waste of time anyway. It was written all over my face and I had been too surprised and distracted to find him in this nearly naked state to make sure that he couldn't

pick it from my thoughts. I wanted to
touch every inch of him. I didn't care
about the Council, this too secretive to
be effective mission, or about a
festival. I could only think of me on
him.

"I'm going to show you where my
wings go." He said.

I saw his full lips moving and heard
some words coming from his direction, but
I was still having trouble focusing. *Ok.
Pull it together.* I coached myself back
to sanity. Focusing on his mouth and
trying to hear words instead of imagining
them on me.

"What was that?"

He held out his hand to me, with a
knowing smile I tried my best not to like
and repeated, "I'm going to show you

where my wings go."

Now? Now he shows me? I shook off the heat that had been building and focused. This was more important than my horny little thoughts. *And besides, we have all night and it's the longest of the year.* I followed him to the seating area and sat across from him.

"Do you remember what you read today about the astral plane?"

"Yes." I answered.

"What is your understanding?"

"It is a place between realms, between waking and sleeping, an intermediary."

Tomas shook his head emphatically. "Yes. The astral plane is where your clothes and weapons go when you shift. It's also where my wings go until I call on them."

I sat back in my chaise. It made perfect sense. I'd never even thought about where what I was carrying went when I shifted. I just accepted it as part of my gift. Really, it was part of my gift. I'd never been able to do anything like that when I wasn't shifting. I just hadn't understood what part before.

"I understand." I said. "Show me."

Tomas turned his back to me. I placed my hands on his back. Feeling the hard smoothness where the wings were earlier today. I could feel a tingling in my fingers and palms as I lay them flat against his back.

"You need to be in front of me." He directed as he turned to face me.

I stood to, placed my hands on his

chest, expecting the tingle that came and pushing past it. I closed my eyes, reaching for his chakra the way that I reached for every being that I became. The usual jolt upon entry did not come, but the surge I always felt after the jolt was stronger than usual. I could feel myself swaying and leaned into his chest a bit to steady myself. I could feel his life energy flowing through his body. Its flow was tumultuous, spilling over the normal lines of flow at every chakra point. The points looked like they were sparking. I started to pull away. It was so powerful; I didn't think I could stand to look at it. Tomas placed his hands over mine, sealing them to his chest.

We pulled in a deep breath together.

Following his energy as it chased itself around his points and feeling his will, I followed him to the astral plane. This intermediary space was just ours. We had created this space with our will, our chakra. The coolness of the plane settled over us. Then as quickly as we left, we were back in the bath. Tomas' wings were outstretched.

Can I touch them. I projected.

He nodded. Turning his back to allow me full access. They were magnificent. I had thought them the color of rust like his hair, but they were many colors ranging from golden to the tone of deepest earth. The softness of the feathers was like so many of the birds that I have become, but the strength underneath the feathers was like nothing I had felt before. I could feel the heavy muscles that ran along the entire top of his wing. The quills that attached to the muscles were thick and sturdy. I was totally engrossed in learning until I felt Tomas shuddering under my touch. With every stroke of his quill, every time I ran my hand over the vane, or touched the follicle he was reacted with an enjoyment that he couldn't conceal.

I reached around the front of his body, exploring with first my left hand then my right. His wings disappeared into the firmament and I found myself pressed against his back. I breathed in his scent, nuzzling into him.

I need you over here. He sent, disappearing and reappearing in the bath noticeably shortless.

You are a showoff. I arrived next to him leaving my new exquisite fighting leathers and my beloved Speedy to wait for me in the space between realms.

Still a quick study. He smiled against my forehead.

17

His body tensed. "Get dressed. Leave Speedy."

"How did you know about Speedy?" I asked. As shocked at the change in demeanor as I was by his knowledge of my hidden weapon.

His only reply was, "Hurry."

Now I could hear them coming too. There were at least four Fae heading this way and 2 of them were heavily armed from the sounds of it. I clothed myself and sat in a chair. The Prince and I were doing a bang up job of pretending to chat casually when the knock came on the door. The Prince looked at me, making a be cool gesture before bidding the group to come in.

And looky here. Who else would be leading the pack but our friend Set. "Dyana, we must escort you to your rooms."

"What is the meaning of this, Set?" The Prince lay a hand on my shoulder as I began to rise.

"The queen has ordered it."

"I will know why, or you will know death, Set. I am in no mood."

"Oh, I can guess your mood." Set

leered.

I was sure he was trying to broadcast one of his little sexual short films, but I was locked up tight - the back door, and all the windows. *Kick rocks, asshole.*

Tomas was rising from his seat. Even with all of this going on, I couldn't help but admire the cut of his clothes against his body. The way his thighs rippled under his pants. *Get a grip, girl.* It was my turn to put a staying hand on him.

"No, Tomas. It is the night of the Solstice. We cannot do this now."

"Listen to your little..." Set trailed off as if he were looking for the word. "...friend? Is that what they're calling it nowadays?" he turned in question to the 3 Fae guards flanking him. One of them smiled a bit, but quickly fixed his face as if just now remembering he faced the Prince.

I did not remove my hand from Tomas as I got up.

"I will know." Tomas emphasized will.

"Yes", Set sneered, "When you speak with your Mommy."

I didn't see, only felt Tomas move. His right hand was on the throat of the Master at Arms before I could register what was happening. Set's feet were dangling in the air as he sputtered, both of his hands holding Tomas' wrist. The soldiers were clearly stunned by both the speed and the actions of the Prince. They looked on in horror unsure of the correct move.

"I. Will. Know." Tomas said calmly, letting Set's feet touch the ground once more.

"The hallow has been stolen." He choked out and looked at me. "Her filthy little scent is all over the chamber."

My room had been searched. My new clothes were strewn about the bedroom and everything was overturned. The torches which I had dubbed Fae Blaze were gone. In their place were every day candles set in holders which were filling with wax. The cooling carafe was gone, and I would bet the tub would no longer stay warm if left alone. The room was stripped of magic. The previous liveliness of the space replaced with the humdrum normalcy of my own realm.

They were serious about this. I reached out gently with my chakra not wanting to get shocked by whatever suppression spell had been placed on the room. My chakra was stilted, but not stopped. I smiled to myself, that little know-it-all, Set, didn't know the extent of my chakra. This room was only strong enough to hold who I'd been when I arrived. He didn't know me then and he sure didn't know me now. I hoped that I would have the chance to show him once Tomas talked to the Queen and got me out of this.

I paced the room, suppressing my chakra and undoing the enhancements I had made to my Fae form since breakfast. Set had been too wrapped up in his half assed victory and his embarrassment at the hands of Tomas to really notice me. That was clear by the poor job he had done of securing my rooms. I felt more than knew that this was my one advantage and I had to keep it.

The night had finally begun to fall, and the palace was alive with music and laughter. Whatever I had been accused of stealing either wasn't important to all of the members of the court or they didn't know about it. Set said that I had stolen a Hallow. That shouldn't be hard for Tomas to disprove since I had no clue what Set was talking about. It wouldn't be hard for me to play innocent, because, ladies and gents, I am in fact without blame.

I went to the window in the bedroom, listening to the voices below. Those were happy voices, untroubled and full of pleasure. I was supposed to be out there dancing with Tomas, not in here.

Finally, there was a knock on my door. I knew it wasn't Tomas and I took my time answering it. Set stood there dressed in fighting leathers, blades on both hips, and strapped across his back. He moved to the side and motioned for me to join him in the hallway. I stepped outside the door, feeling a brief respite at the feeling of the chakra in the hallway.

"Face the door, please." He didn't bother to make the demand sound like a request.

I met his eye before turning towards

the door. He was smiling, a viscous toothy grin that didn't reach his eyes. I felt the ropes of chakra crossing my body, tight across the tops of my breasts, crisscrossing down my back and stomach, and stopping just short of my buttocks. I closed my eyes willing my life energy to stay low so he would not sense it.

"You can never be too careful." He said cheerily as he steered me down the hall.

"Where are we going?" I thought I knew, but I wanted to be sure.

"To meet the Night Queen of course." Set laughed. It was cavernous and thick, carrying down the hall to the front and to the back of us.

I did not know what to expect when we entered the throne room. I had not seen this room on my tour and hadn't bothered to look it up when we were in the library. It was quite small compared to the enormity of the palace in general. The ceilings were as high as the other rooms we had been in, but the room was oddly narrow and squat giving it a fun house feel. I wondered if that was part and parcel of the design - a room made to make an outsider feel off kilter.

The Night Queen was not present when we arrived. I was taken to stand before a dais. The podium like the walls and floors of the palace shone as if they had been polished for my arrival. A throne bejeweled with all manner of precious stones sat in the middle of a dais.

There were several similarly decorated chairs which were not quite as grand to the left and the right of the throne. The fae blaze tossed their light around the rooms, bouncing of the jewels and the floor. It was dazzling to behold.

Set squeezed my binding a bit tighter. "Have you not had enough sightseeing?"

A few of the Night Queen's Court members took their seats. There was good ol' Auntie Z at the left hand of the Queen. I searched for Tomas. The chair to the right of the Queen, which I thought should be his, was empty.

I felt the Night Queen before I saw her. Even Tomas' immense chakra had not readied me for the life energy that surged through the Queen. I didn't have to reach out to her to feel it or see it, it reached out to my shifter senses on its own. It beckoned me to look upon it and survey its glory. She rose from behind the dais, too smoothly to have been walking up steps, and settled in her throne.

The books had been right about her being beauty. Her skin was the color of night, not just the darkness of night, but also the light shining in the night sky. It shimmered. Her eyes were like none I'd ever seen. The cornea was as dark as the pupil and the Fae blaze that landed there seemed to ignite. Her black hair was pulled into a tight, regal bun, beneath a crown of what looked like diamonds. The crown was of simple design, little more than a tiara, but the workmanship was obvious even from where I was standing at least 10 feet away.

Her eyes fell on me and I knew immediately that she was also terrible. The weight of her gaze made me want to squirm and look away, but I knew that would make me look guilty. I waited to be addressed.

"You have stolen from us?" Her voice was both vast and quiet like the sound of waves rolling onto the shore.

"I have not."

The silence stretched on between us. Her skin, her chakra, her presence. All of it was becoming too much to bear.

"I have barely been out of Tomas' sight -" I began to prattle and was halted with a raise of her hand.

"The Prince. Prince Tomas. You

will call him by his name. His name is Prince Tomas."

This was not going well. Set began to pulse the binds making it even harder to focus. I knew this was on purpose. I resisted speaking, even though I could feel the words bubbling up to the surface. I didn't know if I could stop myself if this silence continued.

"I allowed him to choose you, because the sibyl led him to believe you are his mate." She sniffed.

Mate? What was that about.

"Our Realm will celebrate the Winter Solstice as we have done for thousands of years. This news does not leave our Court". The Night Queen's voice carried like a melody through the room. "None of the Council Members are permitted to

leave our Realm. None from the Realm of
Men may enter or exit. Take her to her
quarters." The Queen rose. "And bring
the sibyl to me."

"I didn't steal anything. I don't
even know what there is to steal. I -"

The queen raised her hand again. I
immediately   stopped   speaking.   She
tilted her head slightly to the right as
if she found me interesting, the Fae
blaze still burning in the darkness of
her eyes and she whispered, "Sleep." The
sound of her voice, both soothing and
chilling was the last thing I heard in
that room.

18

I awoke in my room which was no

longer in disarray. Remnants of chakra were still in the air. Whoever had straightened up had used their magic and from what I could tell their magic was in the common caste. The candles on the table were enough to tell me the dampening spell was back on in my ornate prison. I paced the room, convincing myself that Set was behind this and perhaps that other guy from this morning. I did my best to ignore the obvious. Where was Tomas?

At last there was a knock at my door. I rushed to open it. Expecting to see Tomas, I threw it open. Auntie Z was there, flanked by two guards and wearing a wry smile.

"Not who you were expecting?" she sing-songed walking past me into the

sitting room and taking a seat at the now
lifeless table. She motioned for me to
join her.

Well this should be fun. I thought,
not bothering to cover my thoughts. I
didn't think she could read them and
didn't care if she could. I had nothing
to hide and Tomas to protect me.

"Have you had fun swooning after my
nephew?" she asked conversationally. She
motioned to the guards at the door. One
of them came forward. "Bring us tea." She
turned to look at me and questioned,
"Have you had dinner?" She didn't wait
for an answer before adding to her order,
"Bring her dinner."

She turned back to me; a large fake
smile pasted on her face. "Now, tell me

what you've done with it."

I stared at her blankly. "Are you serious."

"Very."

Four attendants entered the room, bustling around us as they set the table. The food smelled delicious and I could always go for tea, so I ate. And she talked, and questioned, and talked some more. The gist of it was I had chased after her nephew like the Realm of Men trollop that I was, taken advantage of his kindness, stolen the Hallow, and was caught red handed. I looked at her over the steaming cup of tea. This was all quite entertaining, really.

"I see" I ventured when I could get a word in edgewise. "And what has Tomas said about all of this?"

"Tomas?" Auntie stirred her tea slowly, squinting her eyes like she was considering where she would go from here with utmost care. She was waiting, biding her time to drop a bomb on me and it was something that she thought would break me. "Oh, you haven't heard. Silly old me. I should have led with that."

"Led with what?" I asked the question she had been dying for me to ask. Better to just plow through this little pageant and get it over with. Maybe she would tire and leave me in peace.

"Tomas has been sent to the Court of Nightfall. They have use of his talents."

"His talents?" I asked.

"There's another stupid, Council lackey there. She has stars in her eyes just like you." She leaned forward as if we were two girlfriends catching up and were just getting to the best part of the gossip, "You see, that's why you were brought here."

I couldn't keep my eyes from widening with surprise as things became clear. I was brought here to take the fall. That little Q & A had been for the attendants and the guards.

All the seeming secrecy and half answered questions were part of their little charade. They hadn't even bothered to fully flush out a plan. They acquired my assistance from the Council with a half-assed story and the promise of coming to their realm. That was all it had taken. That and a gorgeous gigolo who had played me for a fool.

"Oh, I can see from the look on our face that you're finally catching on." She placed her teacup down carefully on the delicate looking dish. "Well" she said in her chipper sing-song voice, "I'll be off now."

I almost wanted her to stay. I'd rather be alone with her than my thoughts.

19

I turned on the water for the bath, sitting on the edge of the tub. The water was steaming hot and I couldn't wait to immerse myself in it. I sunk in in the water, leaning back and closing my eyes. The last hour's events replayed in my mind. The Night Queen's cool assessment of the situation, Auntie Z's visit and our little chat over tea, and the answer to where Tomas had gotten off to. Tamra was right, I didn't know who to trust. Luckily, I was just a danger to myself. I had managed not to harm anyone else with my stupidity.

I allowed myself to remember Tomas' hands on mine. The way our bodies had glowed in the astral plane. I sat up abruptly. I had been in the astral plane. I closed my eyes hoping the dampening spell couldn't keep me from the astral plane. Praying to gods my realm no longer believed in that Set had not blocked access. I called to Tamra. The one person I knew I could trust. I couldn't tell if it was blocked or she wasn't answering. The result was the same. I was on my own.

20

The party raged on outside. The voices of the Fae and the sounds of the musicians almost drowned out the knock at the door. I opened the door to two guards.

"Get dressed." The one on the right said. He had a mean little glint in his eye. "We're taking you to the dungeon."

"You have 5 minutes." The one on the left chimed in.

I closed the door quietly and headed to the bedroom to put on a pair of my new fighting leathers. They had been laundered and were the warmest things in my limited wardrobe. I was pretty sure the dungeon would be cold at night. My hands fell to where Speedy should be. I didn't care how stupid I had been. I was not going to go to anyone's dungeon.

I turned back to the door. They had sent only two guards for me. I would normally be insulted, but not tonight. I only had to get them both in the door and me in the hallway. The dampening spell would do the rest for me.

The hard knock I was expecting came.

"Almost done", I called.

The knock came again immediately, more hammering than knocking. I heard a turning of a key in the door, a physical key. I couldn't believe the luck. They had sent two guards with chakra castes so low they needed to use a key to break the dampening spell on this room. I heard the guards enter the room and poked my head around the door.

"Can't you wait a minute?" I called.

The one with the mean glint in his eye didn't bother to answer, he just charged into the sitting room. The other one was hesitant, entering slowly. They were big, but their life energy was low. Hopefully, Set hadn't sent a crack team to come get me. I was pretty sure he wouldn't have bothered.

The first one came blundering in the room and straight into the vase that I was holding. I didn't even lift it. He ran straight into it. I picked up one of the pieces and flung it at the guard coming in behind him. So far, the noise of the party goers was still drowning us out. As long as I could keep this quiet, I still had a chance. The guard easily dodged the piece of ceramics coming his way - holding both of his arms out and jumping backwards. I snatched the key from his left hand and ran at the door. He was right on my heels and the door was too far. I knelt in front of him abruptly, his speed carried him over my back, tumbling straight towards the doors opening. I grabbed his outstretched legs yanking him back in the room before he could cross the door. I couldn't have anyone outside of the room seeing his flailing arms.

The idiot in the bedroom was making his way towards us, I increased the flow of my chakra allowing it to spill over the points, touching the cells flanking the points of the flow. I pushed the air at them both, infusing it with force. The furniture and delicate dishes flew at the guards before the wind caught up and they went barreling towards the far wall of the bedroom. I didn't stay to watch them hit it.

I poked my head into the hallway. No one there. They really didn't think much of me, huh? I turned the key in the lock and tucked it above the door. I could hear them scrambling towards the door on the other side. They would have several hours before anyone would be able to hear them over the sounds of the festival.

I shored up my mind and made my way through the palace shifting into the attendant who had bought tea to Auntie Z. I dampened my chakra to common caste and headed for the nearest exit trying desperately to remember the course Tomas had taken me through that morning. I rounded the corner and saw four guards stationed at the palace door and wondered why I had not anticipated this. Of course, there would be security. It was a wonder this wasn't more of it. But the guards didn't seem to be concerned about security in the least. I could smell the wine before I saw it.

I decided to go for it. Putting my head down, I rushed through them like I was on a mission.

"Dana, where are you going in such a hurry." One of the guards called after me.

"Where they tell me." I said good naturedly as I rushed on hoping the voice, I gave sounded close enough to pass for their friend.

The laughter behind me told me that I was safe for now. I rushed into the streets, mixing into the crowd as quickly as I could. I couldn't afford for the real Dana to appear and bring up questions.

Once I knew that I was thoroughly hidden in the crowd, I chanced another shift. This time into a Fae I spotted just as I was leaving the castle, I danced my way through the crowd. I just needed to create enough space to take flight. I knew exactly where I was going. The Night Queen had shut down all means of transportation to my Realm, but not even she could control the Anubis.

Flying in the Fae form was delightful even in this situation. The feeling of soaring in a form so close to my resting form was exhilarating beyond anything I'd ever felt in flight. I passed a few other Fae in the sky their wings taking on the purple and pink hues of the solstice. They all soared right past be, not even acknowledging my presence in the sky. I rushed on fighting the need to slow to a more leisurely pace and enjoy this moment, these sights, and the smell of whatever the Fae were cooking in the pyres scattered through the cities' parks.

I soared closer to the area of protection and began my descent being careful not to get close enough for that the Hell Cats to catch my scent before I was prepared for them. The moment my feet touched the ground, I sensed his presence. Set was here.

21

I kept my eyes closed, concentrating on the flow of chakra allowing it to run wilder and more forcefully. The light in my mind's eye began chasing itself through the points, skittering around the corners sloppily and sloshing onto the cells around the points. I could feel him closing in from behind as any coward would.

"I know there's no sneaking up on you." His tone was equal parts suspicion and amusement.

"Enough with the ear jokes already." I poked the bear hoping that he would keep running his mouth giving me more time to transform my body.

"Surely, you must know that I sensed the changes in you the moment you started making them."

I made no reply. He sensed the change but was stupid enough to let me continue powering up. I didn't think so. He sensed a change, but not this.

He was no less arrogant than the first time we met. I felt him snaking around the barrier to my thoughts. His presence in my head was like oil on water, floating at the surface unable to go any further. I could feel him pressing, but I wasn't giving an inch.

I felt him withdraw from my mind. I faced him. He was only about 4 feet away from me. He was wearing his fighting leathers. His hand rested gently on the hilt of a broad sword.

"Are you planning to use that thing on me?" I looked at him expectantly and plastered the biggest smile I could muster.

He smiled back. I think it was a genuine smile which only made it that much more appalling. "I am going to enjoy carving you up." Pulling his sword from its sheath he continued in a low voice, "The Prince can have his pick of the pieces."

Oh, this was the game he was playing. It was going to take more than the mention of Tomas to make me fall apart. His little girlfriend had already played that song and I was over that tune.

"I think I know what parts you'll choose." I teased, running my fingers lightly over my lips. "I see how you look at me."

His eyes narrowed in disgust, "You certainly cannot read the room, Dyana."

It was my turn to laugh. The guy did have some pretty funny barbs, too bad he couldn't stop being a bastard.

He stepped closer affecting a casual posture, but I could see he was positioning to strike, sense him gathering his life force. I could see the path of the line of chakra in his body. The current thick, full, and bright rushed around the loop.

I raised my hand slowly, calling Speedy from the cosmos between the worlds. I could sense my curling blade coming towards me and opened my hand to receive it. My fingers closed along Speedy's brass hilt. Her two blades curled up to half their length about 2.5 feet long.

"Learned some new tricks, I see." Set released the guise of casual conversationalist, shifting his weight to his toes and bending his knees.

"I wouldn't call them new." I mused. I could see I was getting under his skin, so I continued, "I mean, really. Is there anything new underneath the sun?"

Set lunged forward, swinging his sword at my midsection. He really did intend to slice me up. I dodged his first lunge and allowed him to reset.

"I thought you were learning to like me." I side stepped his second swing. My movements in this form with this level of chakra were so quick it was like teleporting. It was dizzying to me, I wondered if it was having a similar effect on him. I had begun this fight thinking there was a fair chance that I could get out of this, but I should have trained in this body. The quickness of my Fae form was disorienting. This could end badly.

I felt him at my back and shifted away quickly not wasting time trying to figure out where he would strike. I needed to get distance. I flicked my wrist fully extending Speedy and began the dance.

I whipped the curling blade out, the sand billowing as the blades kissed the surface of the ground and whirled back into the air arcing behind me and over my head. I could feel him coming before I saw him. Whirling to my right, I pulled the blades through the air in front of me. The dispersing of the sand under my blades creating a smoky cloud around me. I didn't have to see Set; I could feel him. His chakra pulsed within him, his anger stalling the flow, throwing him off kilter as we fought. He chased me, barely managing to stay out of reach of the blades.

I weaved to my left lifting my right arm overhead allowing the blades to uncurl their full 5 feet, quickly snapping my wrist. I caught the right of his neck. I couldn't see the welts forming where my blades had struck, but imagining his blood running down his neck made me smile. He threw his sword down and rushed me. I flung Speedy straight out aiming for his eyes, but he threw up his arm, allowing Speedy to wrap around his forearm and pulled.

I lurched forward, unwilling to let go of my weapon, and his fist connected with my jaw in an explosion of pain. The hit was head on. The force of it spinning my body, head leading the way, to the right. I thudded to the ground.

He stood over me, the colors of the eclipse framing his form. He pressed his left foot into my right wrist making me release Speedy. He threw his head back, barking a laugh at the moon. Tossing his sword aside, he knelt over me, pulled a smaller knife from his digging one of his knees into each shoulder.

"I think I'll start with your stupid ears." He spat.

That is when the first Hell Catt pounced on him. Set's knife skittered across the ground. He let out a guttural, wordless shout of anger as he wrestled with the giant feline. I could smell Set's blood in the air. It seemed he was losing this fight. The other Hell Catts moved in smelling prey. One nuzzled my hand as it stalked past me to join its pack.

I let out a shuddering breath in front of the Anubis. "Take me home".

I felt the pull of the Anubis in my stomach first. A gentle, but firm tug

that was followed by the headiness that
I was starting to be accustomed to. I
pictured my home in my mind's eye. My
fireplace, the comfy leather chair where
Tamra dispersed most of her advice, and
my collection of Scotch on my beloved
stainless-steel bar cart. *Take me home*,
I broadcast over and over again.

23

I sat in the park, watching Santa's
Elves try to corral in the last of the
skaters. It was Christmas Eve and there
wasn't as much traffic on the ice rink,
but there was still enough for a laugh or
two.

I had not been debriefed yet and
today was the day. I wasn't even sure

what there was to tell. There was some sort of Hallow the Fae, all or some of them, had gone through great pains to make seem like members of the Council had stolen. I had no idea why, not a clue what the Hallow was, and was likewise as useless when it came to what the Hallow did. This debriefing would last about 15 seconds.

I took off my gloves so I could feel the hot chocolate in my hands. A small piece of linen fell out of my pocket as I tried to shove them in there. That was odd. I wasn't really one for carrying scraps of linen around. I turned the piece around to study it. Written in red was the word **Remember**.

<<<<>>>>

Printed in Poland
by Amazon Fulfillment
Poland Sp. z o.o., Wrocław